Death's Ferryman Rides a Harley

Death's Ferryman Rides a Harley

Virginia McCausland

First Paperback Edition: January 2022

Book and cover design: Virginia McCausland

Cover Images: Deposit Photos
Part One Composite Image: Bench © Zothen/Adobe Stock,
Spotlight © Feaspb/Shutterstock
Part Two Image: Man on Harley © Tee Tee Photo
Part Three Image: Silhouette of girl at sunset © Chuabanrai Ekawat

Author Photo: Ray Hudson

Paperback ISBN 978-1-7776778-0-0
E-book ISBN 978-1-7776778-1-7

Website: www.virginiamccausland.com

For my Muses Mary-Lou and Cai

"We dance for laughter, we dance for tears, we dance for madness, we dance for fears, we dance for hopes, we dance for screams, we are the dancers, we create the dreams."
— Albert Einstein

Part One
Clara

Chapter One

What is death anyway? If Einstein's theory of relativity holds true, everything is pure energy. Absolutely everything. The universe, the galaxy, the earth, and all the cells in our bodies. That makes us immortal. Doesn't it?

I found myself in a position to explore Einstein's theories about time when I nodded off to sleep for a few minutes while waiting for the bus. I awoke to the roar of a motorcycle vibrating through me. Exhaust lingered in the air. A leather-clad biker straddled a Harley on the street in front of me. I recognized the distinct popping sound a Harley makes when it idles as my dad tinkered with an old Harley from time to time. The biker wore tight jeans with a Harley-Davidson belt buckle. In his hand, he held my kaleidoscope, a handcrafted triangular cylinder made of mirrors and wheels decorated with beads and crystals, not the plastic dollar store kind. My boyfriend Peter gave me the kaleidoscope for my birthday, and I wanted it back.

"Hey babe," he said, pointing the kaleidoscope at me. "Is this yours?" His voice reminded me of chocolate, dark and smooth.

"Yes, that's mine." When I stood, my legs buckled, and I had to sit down again. The trees, the houses, and the parked cars blurred together. I gripped the bench and waited until everything came back into focus. My head felt woozy like it often did when I stayed awake all night at a sleepover. But I hadn't been to a sleepover. I'd been waiting for the bus and for Peter, who promised to meet me. Jagged streams of light flickered before my eyes like a nauseating optical headache. I clutched my stomach and prayed I wouldn't heave my guts all over the sidewalk.

The biker turned off his hog, lifted his leg over the seat, and stepped onto the curb. "Hey babe, are you okay?" he asked.

I licked my lips and tasted chocolate. Strange, the taste of his voice settled my stomach. "Yeah, it's nothing." I didn't want to get into a conversation with this guy who kept calling me babe, but I did want my kaleidoscope back. I held out my hand. "The kaleidoscope. It's mine."

He ignored me and pointed the kaleidoscope at my face, a gesture I found rude and disconcerting.

"Cool kaleidoscope," he said while twirling the wheels. "I found it in the middle of the street. You're lucky no one ran over it." After spinning the wheels one more time, he handed it to me.

While I checked the kaleidoscope for cracks, the biker walked over to the coin-operated newspaper box and banged on the lock with his fist. Without putting a coin in the slot, he opened the door and pulled out a newspaper. He flipped the paper open and sat beside me. I scooted over on the bench as far as I could. Einstein's biography lay between us, the book I borrowed from the library for a school project.

The dude looked twenty or so. I smelled spice, *Old Spice*. My father's aftershave. A mop of windblown hair, red, the flaming kind, like my sister Lucy's stuck out this way and that. Curly too, just like Lucy's. He tucked a curl behind one ear, pierced with a gold hoop, a snake swallowing its tail. Thick eyelashes, the kind I'd wished I'd been born with, framed his eyes. Day-old stubble shadowed his cheeks, and a hint of mechanic's grease blackened his fingernails. Not as cute as my boyfriend Peter, but not bad at all. Really, he didn't look hard like some bikers, but my gut told me to be cautious.

I looked through the kaleidoscope and, by some miracle, found it all in one piece. Not one cracked mirror or broken crystal. It didn't make sense. A kaleidoscope this fragile would have shattered if I'd dropped it or if it rolled off the curb and onto the pavement. I wondered, did the biker find it or take it? "You know, I don't remember dropping it."

"You were asleep." He rested his arm, a muscular bicep framed by a black leather vest behind me. I crossed my legs to make as much room as I could between us.

My face flushed at the thought of the dude seeing me sleeping on the bench like a homeless person. I looked down at his leather boots, at his muddy heels and scuffed toes. "I may have nodded off for a few minutes," I confessed under my breath.

"That's the best part of sleep. Don't you think Einstein would agree?" With his index finger, he tapped the cover of Einstein's biography sitting between us.

I gave him a sideways glance. I was curious how a guy like him could know anything about Einstein. I didn't know many people interested in Einstein, let alone were familiar with his peculiar sleep habits. "Yes, I think Einstein would agree. He used to doze for a few moments off and on during the day. All his great theories came from those short catnaps that flooded his mind with images and solutions to his work."

He picked up the book and ruffled the pages like my friend Marty does when he speed reads. "Did your mind open a flood gate?" he asked.

"No. Well, yes. Now that I think about it, I do remember a dream."

"Have you noticed that dreams can feel like they are going on for hours when in fact, they only last a few minutes? Do you think dreams fit Einstein's theories about time?"

Einstein believed the past, present, and future were simultaneous, but I'd never related dream time to that theory. Maybe the biker had a point. "You mean dreams have a timeless quality," I said.

"A dream exists outside of time," he said.

"Like if you travel at the speed of light, you end up in a state of timelessness."

He smiled. "Imagine that. No time."

"Yes, imagine that." I didn't know if I should be impressed or wary of this biker who could carry on a conversation about Einstein's theories. Still, I couldn't help being a little excited to be talking to someone interested in Einstein and his work.

"Cool guy, that Einstein." He handed me the book.

"Yes, very cool." I tucked the book and my Kaleidoscope into my bag, still where I left it, by my feet. Who knows, someone could have stolen my bag while I slept.

When I moved to stand, the biker said, "Did you solve any mathematical problems in your dream?"

"Well…" I hesitated to tell this total-stranger-biker-dude my dream, but he had a friendly air I found hard to resist. And, seriously, the guy had some smarts, or he wouldn't be able to discuss Einstein with me. Still, I'm not the kind of girl to blab to a stranger, let alone a biker, but his smooth as chocolate voice compelled me to say, "Yes, as a matter of fact, I did solve some mathematical equations in my dream. I saw geometric shapes swirling in a vortex."

"Like looking through a kaleidoscope," he said.

"Yes, sort of. I found the geometric shapes and colors mesmerizing, that is until mathematical equations flew like spears out of the vortex toward me. I felt under attack. If I didn't solve the equations correctly, I would be impaled or something worse. I shouted out the answers to the equations, but they came at me faster and faster, with each one becoming harder to solve than the last one. I must have answered an equation wrong because everything went dark, and I fell screaming into an abyss. Thank God the sound of your Harley woke me before I hit the bottom. You know, you can die if that happens in a dream."

"Really? I didn't know that." His voice hummed with skepticism.

"Seriously, you can die. The shock can make your heart stop."

"Well then, I guess I saved your life."

"I don't know about that. I'm sure I would have awakened before that happened." Using the bench for balance, I pulled myself to my feet. When I found the dizziness had passed, I slipped my bag over my arm, stepped off the curb, and scanned the street.

Diffused light shone through the pine trees, creating long shadows like arms reaching out to me from another world. Where was the bus and where was Peter? Both were late. Very late.

I unzipped the lower pocket on my cargo pants and dug out the watch my father gave me for Christmas. He made a point of telling me it cost a bundle and warned me not to leave it lying around like I did some of my other things. It had a gold expansion band and the figure of a dancer carved in crystal on the watch's face. I tapped the face with my finger, placed it to my ear, and listened. Silence. I groaned. The second hand wouldn't budge. I checked my cellphone, dead like my watch.

"Excuse me. Do you know what time it is?" I asked the biker-dude, now absorbed by the want ads.

He lowered the newspaper, and, for an instant, his eyes, dark brown with amber flecks, met mine. "It's not time yet," he said.

A cold sensation crept through me. I swallowed the lump in my throat and debated whether I should run away or ask him what he meant by "it's not time yet." I took a chance and asked, "What do you mean it's not time? For the bus?"

"You missed it," he said and turned a page. "Whoa, look at that. What a beauty."

I sat and peered over his shoulder at the ad for a Harley, a low-rider with lots of chrome, high handlebars, dual exhaust pipes, and leather saddlebags back and front. I didn't know much about motorcycles, but the picture underlined by his thumb did look drool-worthy.

"Wicked." I tried to sound interested, but really, I wasn't.

"Awesome drag bars…" he said.

"Yeah, they're cool, but I couldn't have missed the bus. I was sitting right here waiting for it. I didn't hear it come by."

"How could you? You were dead to the world." His eyes silenced me.

I took a moment to collect my thoughts. "I must have been tired, dead tired, or I wouldn't have fallen asleep. That's not like me."

"Hard day at school?" he asked.

I couldn't remember what happened at school or what I ate for breakfast, for that matter. Grapefruit and toast? Eggs? Yogurt and bananas? I tasted donuts. The taste triggered something in my rattled brain, and the memories came back little by little, like sand sifting through an hourglass.

Before school, I met Peter at the coffee shop. We were going to skip band class and spend time celebrating my birthday, eating donuts for breakfast. You see, I never eat donuts because I'm a dancer and well, they're too fattening. Anyhow, we fought and went to the band practice anyway. Lately, he'd been acting strange, not talking, not looking me in the eyes, and avoiding me in the hallway, usually when I saw him speaking to Isabel.

All day my stomach churned with the he's-going-to-dump-me blues. During my exam in English class, I tried to calm my stomach by eating pieces of a granola bar hidden in my pencil case. I kept looking at the clock. Time moved at a snail's pace. Each minute dragged on like ten minutes. I freaking failed that exam. I couldn't wait for the bell to ring so I could get the hell out of there.

The biker waited for an answer. I didn't know what to say. Panic gripped me. There were no more memories, only a sense of dread.

What was I worried about? My audition? Maybe. Lucy? No. I never worried about what she was up to. Marty? Could be.

He had so much crap to deal with at home and Cindy, poor Cindy. Some girls were mean to her, and I had promised to be her friend, but, well, she didn't make it easy for me. As for Peter, I worried about him and us all the time. But it wasn't my relationship with Peter that had me on edge. It was something else. Something more frightening than losing Peter. But what? The memory hovered out of reach like a forgotten word on the tip of my tongue.

The biker-dude's eyes never left me while I mulled over what happened during the day, so I said, "Yeah, I guess it was a hard day." My voice sounded weak, almost a whisper.

I stood. I sat, I stood and sat again. Something felt wrong. Anxiety gnawed at the pit of my stomach. I needed to know when the next bus was due, so I asked him again. "Do you have a watch? It's important. You see, I was waiting for someone. He promised to go to my audition with me. It's a professional group, not a school production, and it would mean so much if I won the part. I want to be famous someday. If Peter doesn't come soon, I'll have to go without him. I don't want to be late, but I really want him to come to the audition because he's my good luck charm. You have a watch, don't you? Or a cellphone? Both of mine are dead." When I'm anxious or worried, I talk fast. I even babble like an idiot to a complete stranger.

The biker settled back and folded the newspaper. He tucked the paper between us and rummaged through his pockets. "I haven't had much need for a watch lately, but I think there's one in here somewhere."

He placed a stack of loose change, a gold ring, and a hospital band on top of the folded newspaper. I glanced at the coins and quickly calculated how much he had—my quirky talent with numbers guaranteed me an "A" in math. "You know you have nine dollars and ninety-five cents in change. Almost ten bucks."

"That would be about right."

"And two, two-dollar bills." The bills were crisp and in mint condition, except for the fold in the middle. "I hope you're not going to spend them." He regarded me with a frown, like he didn't know that two-dollar bills were a collector's item.

"No, I won't be spending them now." He folded the bills and put them back in his pocket. The gold ring, he slipped on his finger. I picked up the hospital band. Somebody cut it in half, but I could still make out the name and date. "Billy Monroe, St Vincent's hospital, September 27th." The year had faded. "No way. That's my name. I mean, Monroe is my last name. I'm Clara Monroe."

"I know."

Chilled, I rubbed the goosebumps on my arms. "How could you know my name? I've never met you before."

With his boot, he pointed to the stitching on my bag. I'd forgotten my mother had embroidered my name on it.

"What about the watch? You said you had one."

"I do… somewhere." He pulled out a gold pocket watch from a pocket inside his leather vest and dangled it in front of me. "Timing is everything, isn't it? I'm afraid it stopped working a long time ago."

I took the pocket watch and examined it. It had a big face with the image of a Harley in the center. "Look, it stopped on September 27th, the same day you were in the hospital."

Billy nodded as if remembering something from a long time ago. "Yes, that's when it stopped, alright."

The watch looked familiar. I'd seen one similar to Billy's

somewhere. I shivered. My mother had the same pocket watch locked in her keepsake box. Once, when I stayed home from school with the flu, she took the pocket watch out of her jewelry box, wound it, and placed it to her ear. When I asked her about it, she let me listen to it. It chirped when it ticked, in a rhythmic pattern, three fast ticks and two slow ticks. I didn't get a close look at it because she took it away and locked it in her special box.

"Hey, my mom owns a watch like yours. Freaky, you have the same last name and the same watch. What are the chances of that happening?"

"Nothing happens by chance," he said.

"Nothing?"

"Well, nothing important."

I was beginning to think I was having a conversation with biker Yoda. What did Billy mean by nothing happens by chance? Something about Billy made me uneasy, and it wasn't just the biker outfit and the crazy answers to my questions. I sprang to my feet, ready to hightail it out of there when I heard the bus's brakes hiss as it came around the corner.

I grabbed my bag and stood beside the bus stop, but the bus zipped by without stopping. I waved my arms and ran behind it, screaming for it to wait. I'd gone less than half a block when I had to stop. If I took another step, I'd faint or just plain come apart, bit by bit. Geometric patterns of colored light swirled before my eyes. Sometimes, when Dad drank a little too much, he'd say, "Leave me alone, baby. I'm discombobulated." I had to be coming down with a virus or something. That would explain why I fell asleep at the bus stop and why my stomach hurt.

With silly-putty-legs, I walked back to the bench and slumped down. My arms and legs ached, so did my head. I couldn't let a flu bug stop me from going to my audition. I had to get this part. I just had to. I stretched my legs, kicked off my sandals and pointed my toes, and waited for the dizziness to fade.

"You didn't think the bus would stop, did you?" Billy asked.

"Why wouldn't it. The bus wasn't full."

"He didn't see you," Billy said.

"He must be blind. He didn't see you either," I said.

"I'm not waiting for the bus."

Right. I knew that. Billy came on his Harley. "Why are you sitting here?"

"I'm waiting."

"Waiting for what?" I asked.

"The right time."

The hair on the back of my neck spiked with the eerie sensation you get when you're walking home alone at night in the dark. My cellphone was dead. There wasn't another person on the street, and I was sitting all alone at the bus stop with a biker who talked like Yoda.

I looked past Billy toward the streaks of red and gold brightening the horizon. The shadows and the sun's position in the sky meant it was a lot later than four in the afternoon. I rummaged in my pocket and pulled out my watch to see if, by some miracle, it had started working again. No luck. Still dead.

"Perhaps the watch needs a new battery," he said. "Let me see." He held out his hand, and before I could stop myself, I let the watch fall into his palm.

"I hope it's not broken. My father gave it to me."

"Hmm… A new battery won't bring this watch back to life.

Look, it's cracked." He tapped the glass, and sure enough, I saw a faint crack across the crystal dancer.

"Oh, I didn't notice that. God, what'll I tell my dad? I wonder when it broke."

"It stopped yesterday afternoon, May 12th, at 4:43 pm," he said.

"Yesterday! That's not right. Today is May 12th."

"May 12th was yesterday."

"May 12th is today. I know because I have an audition today, and it's my birthday."

Billy pointed to the date in the newspaper. "See? May 13th."

I snatched the newspaper and stared at the date. "What's happening? May 13th, is that today or tomorrow?"

"As you see it, tomorrow, as I see it, well, it doesn't matter. Yesterday, today, tomorrow, it's all the same to me. What matters is now."

I scrunched the newspaper. "But…but if it's May 13th, I've missed my audition. I wanted the part more than anything in the world. I have an audition for the role of Liesl in *The Sound of Music*. There were two call-backs, Ashley and myself, and I know I can beat her. I've had the words to *Sixteen Going on Seventeen* memorized since I turned five. I'm sixteen today, I mean yesterday, anyway, I can sing and dance. And I know how it is to have a guy kiss you one day and dump you the next. That's a long story, before I met Peter. God, what's happened to him? Why is he's so late? I hope, I hope he's not thinking of…"

"Of dumping you?"

"A girl always worries a guy will dump her, especially if the boy she's going with is the hottest guy in the whole school. There are so many other girls he could hang with, and if he'd been here, he would have awakened me. I couldn't have slept on the bench all night, or my parents would have come looking for me. God, I'm discombobulated. I need to go home."

I stood and grabbed my bag. "Nice meeting you, Billy," I said without looking back at him.

"And you, Clara," I heard him say.

I walked toward the streetlight and stopped when I saw, piled at the base, a mound of cellophane-wrapped carnations, lilies, and roses. A pair of ballet shoes lay cradled between the bouquets. I squatted by a picture leaning against a potted yellow mum—a picture of me. My dad took it when I received an award for *The Most Promising Dancer*. In the picture, I wore a black sequined dress. It made me look and feel so mature. Who put the photo here and why?

Billy squatted beside me. "It's okay."

"No, it's not." I wanted to vomit from that sickening sensation I'd get from practicing too many pirouettes in a row. "This is crazy. I'm not dead."

He stood and offered me his hand. I shook my head. "I'm not dead," I said again and stumbled to my feet. "I'm not sure what happened, but I gotta go. I need to tell them it's all a big mistake."

"It's not a mistake, "Billy said.

"How would you know? Unless this is a joke. Well, if it is, it isn't funny. Peter put you up to it, didn't he? And Marty. It has to be the best trick so far. Who came up with the idea to use my last name on your hospital band? Nice touch. And the watch? Did Lucy get it for you? Who are you, an actor?"

"It's time." His hand brushed mine.

I slapped it away. "Back off, creep. You're crazy if you think I'm going anywhere with you." With trembling legs, I turned and ran.

I hoped Billy wouldn't follow me.

"When you're ready, call me," Billy said. "And by the way, happy birthday."

I raced across the street to Al's Grocery, where I could wait and watch for the next bus. I needed to lose this biker and the cruel joke someone staged by the streetlight.

I heard the roar of a Harley kick starting and smelled a whiff of gasoline. When I looked over my shoulder, a streak of light flashed by.

Chapter Two

I opened the door to Al's Grocery and almost hurled from the stench of garlic sausage, curdled milk, and stale freezer compartments. On a hot day, the odors could make Superman gag. Since Al's Grocer is the only store in the neighborhood and close to the school, it's our favorite hangout. Outside on the patio, Al set up picnic tables and benches for the students so we would hang there. There would be no more vacations to Palm Springs for Al and his wife without our business.

Voices drifted from the patio. Someone said my name. I closed the door and listened. Some words I could make out and some I couldn't. My name, I heard clearly. It's weird how I could hear my name when other words were barely audible. I recognized the voices and inched my way around the corner.

Ashley, Tina, and Isabel huddled together underneath the awning. I edged closer to the patio and ducked behind the open dumpster to listen. The nasty brew of rotting garbage buzzed with flies. I clutched my stomach. Staying behind the dumpster without barfing would be tough, but if I wanted to hear what they were saying about me, I had to suck it up. I lifted the hem of my T-shirt and buried my nose in the folds before peering around the dumpster.

"We have to stick together and make sure our stories match." Ashley brushed her hair back from her forehead.

I couldn't help but notice her tangled hair and plain face. Ashley never left the house without make-up. She's the kind of girl who won't answer her cellphone with an eyelash out of place. Strange to see her hair looking so messy.

Ashley scratched the zits on her forehead and made one bleed. She wiped her bloodied finger on her jeans. "Are you guys as itchy as me?" she asked.

"Worse," Tina scratched the welt on her arm.

"Try baking soda," Isabel said. Like Ashley, Isabel had zits on her face. Or were those bug bites? I clamped my hand over my mouth to keep from laughing out loud. What if those spots were lice bites? Wouldn't that be divine justice for all the crap they have dished out about me?

"Do you think anyone saw us?" Tina smoothed her Spandex top over her skinny jeans. Yesterday's outfit. Wasn't that proof that today was May 12th? The class fashion snob never wore the same clothes two days in a row. She wants to be a model, but I don't think she has the goods. For one thing, she's not tall or thin enough. The coolest designer jeans, high heel sandals, or lace camisoles can't change that.

"I'm sure no one saw us," Isabel said, "and I don't think Cindy will ever be able to tell. It doesn't look good for her."

"Oh God, what if she wakes up?" Tina glanced towards my hiding place. I hugged the Dumpster.

"If Cindy wakes up, we'll deal with it if and when it happens," Isabel said.

Wakes up? What did they mean? Was Cindy sick or hurt? Was she going to die? I didn't remember anything happening to Cindy at school. Lately, we've been walking home together, not because she is my friend or anything but because I promised to protect her. Today, she had to walk home alone because of my audition. What if something happened to her because I couldn't be there for her? I wanted to jump out from behind the dumpster and ask the girls what happened, but I couldn't. My questions would silence them, so I held my place and listened.

Isabel kept touching her nose stud, a diamond chip. She pierced her nose last week. It still looked raw and sore, but she looked as good without make-up as she did with it, unlike Ashley. I was insanely jealous of Isabel. All the girls were. She had it all, dark eyes with full lashes, high cheekbones, and long black hair as shiny and straight as shoestring licorice. Her skin-tight tank top and white Capri's showed off her to-die-for figure and her ankle dragon tattoo. No wonder all the guys drooled over her, including Peter. But beauty isn't everything, and he broke up with her after a few months and asked me out. The one thing I know for sure is that Isabel would like to deck me for taking Peter away from her.

"The only one who suspects something is Peter, and he's in so much trouble right now he won't say anything. I can guarantee that," Isabel said.

Peter in trouble? For a second time, I forced myself to stay hidden behind the dumpster. I swallowed my fears and listened. If

I approached them, they wouldn't tell me anything.

"Oh God, Peter knows." Tina paled beneath her spray-on tan.

"Chill, will you." Isabel placed her arm around Tina's shoulder. "Peter knows to stay quiet. I've seen to that."

"What if he doesn't?" Ashley's hands were shaking. "Maybe… maybe we should come clean."

"Are you stupid?" Isabel said through clenched teeth. "If you say one word, I'll tell everyone about how you came to own that cute little black bra you're wearing."

The black strap from Ashley's bra had slipped halfway to her elbow. She pulled it back onto her shoulder and tucked it under her tank top.

I'd had enough. What did these bitches do? "Hey," I yelled and walked toward them, but they continued talking as if they hadn't heard me. I took a deep breath and let it out slowly.

"I think we should leave Clara some flowers," Tina said. A chocolate stream dripped from her Fudgsicle onto her hand and dotted her cami with brown spots. Her tongue darted, snake-like, in and out of her mouth to wipe the chocolate from her lips. Not a pretty sight for a fashion queen.

"Don't bother," I said. "I'm on to your petty joke." It was a joke, wasn't it? I had to admit they were doing a convincing act of ignoring me.

Isabel crinkled a bag of salt and vinegar potato chips. My mouth watered as I watched her shovel a handful into her mouth. "Want one?" She offered the bag to Ashley, who waved it away. Before Tina could put her hand into the bag, I snatched one. She didn't flinch. Now that scared me. I crunch the chip between my teeth. The salt and the vinegar made my cheeks pucker. I must be alive. Or was I? I could smell Al's grocer and taste a potato chip, but I couldn't make the girls hear or see me. Is this what happens when you die? I didn't want to believe it. I couldn't be dead. I just couldn't. To keep from freaking out, I told myself I'm energy. I'm not dead. Just like Einstein said.

"Al has some nice bouquets." Ashley's eyes filled with tears.

"C'mon, Ashley, don't get soft on us." Isabel pushed a stray curl from Ashley's eye. "We're a team. We have to stick together."

"I know, but it's just that Clara and I were best friends once. God, I feel awful."

Right. My BFF. What a fake. For years, we were closer than sisters. We dressed alike, talked alike, took the same dance classes, and had sleepovers every weekend. Everything was cool as long as Ashley commanded all the leads and won all the awards. The moment I began to beat her at the dance festivals, she spread rumors about me. Nasty ones. What a poor sport. Now we hardly speak to one another. When Peter dumped Isabel for me, she befriended Ashley, and together with Tina, they gave me grief whenever they could get away with it. They laughed behind my back, ignored me when I spoke to them, and generally made life miserable at school. Peter kept me sane. A bullied girl can hold her head high when dating the hottest and most popular guy at school. The same couldn't be said for Cindy, who wilted every time someone said something nasty to her. Poor Cindy. She endured their snide remarks all year and without one friend to confide in.

"Yeah, we'd better do the flower thing. I don't want people to think we don't care," Isabel said.

The flower thing? So, touching. If only they could hear me. I'd tell them what I really thought of their stupid flowers.

Isabel took a sip from her bottle of cherry-flavored spring water. Tina grabbed the bottle from Isabel's hand. She took a long drink, finished it, and handed it back to Isabel without saying thanks. Isabel pursed her lips and narrowed her eyes. I'd seen that look many times when Isabel played basketball. She tossed the bottle into the recycling bin ten feet away. She scored. Isabel always scored. "Let's see if Al has any bouquets," she said and led them around the corner and into the store.

Angry and confused, I walked back to the bus stop and sat on the bench.

What a nightmare! I've had some odd dreams before. Once, I woke in the middle of a dream and discovered I was still dreaming, a dream within a dream. But never anything this creepy. I couldn't tell if I was awake, still sleeping, or dead. Oh god, I hope not dead. Maybe death is a never-ending dream. Like life. "Row, row, row your boat; life is but a dream." And death too.

Whatever, dead, alive, or still sleeping. I decided to forgo my audition and walk home. My legs shook as I walked across the street to the path leading down the embankment on the other side of the bus stop. All my senses were on alert. Was I being followed? I'd never felt so spooked. I didn't usually take the shortcut through the forest and across the river this late in the day, but it was still light enough to see, and I needed to get home as fast as possible. My house sat on the opposite side of the river, at the top of the embankment.

The moment I stepped over the ridge, black spots floated before my eyes. I rubbed my eyes to clear the haze that blended the sky, trees, and shrubs into a watercolor wash. I gripped a tree branch and waited for the dizzy spell to end. It didn't, so I pushed on as best I could with the ground pulsating under my feet. I kept my eyes glued to the shoreline and the path leading up the hill to my backyard.

This part of the river is not as wild as it is further north of the city, but it swells at this time of year, and the rapids can be dangerous. When I keep my window open during the summer months, I can hear the sound of the rapids breaking over the rocks, a lullaby to soothe me to sleep.

The river has flatwater sections, some shallow but others so deep that wading is not safe as there is a strong undertow. When the river is shallow during the summer, it is possible to cross to the other side by stepping from boulder to boulder, but even in hot, dry weather, the boulders can be slippery with moss. Most of the time, I use the log that fell across the river from shore to shore in a windstorm two years ago. It can be dangerous, but I can use the branches attached to the trunk for handholds and stability.

I inched my way down to the river's edge and walked along the shore, a sliver of sand and rocks. The water lapped to the shoreline, where I found the log bridge. I wasn't afraid, as I used the trunk countless times to cross the river, and I'd never known the log to wobble. Most of the time, traveling across the tree trunk was as safe as walking across the kitchen floor. Still, I tested the log with my foot to make sure. While the tree trunk felt steady, I became light-headed and dizzy.

My forehead felt moist and cool from the water spray. I didn't have a fever, yet the urge to vomit increased with each passing moment. I stepped onto the log and placed one foot in front of the other. Halfway across the river, my foot slipped on a slick patch of moss. Staggering, I pawed the air and fell. The river, swollen from the spring runoff, rose in a vortex toward me. It pulled me under the water one moment and tossed me up on the crest of a wave the next. The sharp edge of a granite slab jutting out of the water stabbed me in my back. I grabbed a branch from a tree leaning over the water, but it broke. The undertow sucked me under again, and I came up to the surface into a whirlpool. I spiraled around and around while flailing my arms and legs, but I couldn't break free. Exhausted, I let go and found myself drawn into the center of the eddy, where I lost consciousness.

I awoke as if from a deep sleep and found myself back on the bench by the bus stop. I kept thinking, what day is it? The 12th or the 13th. Then the whole devastating truth of what had happened to me came back in one overwhelming rush. The bench by the bus stop, Billy on his Harley, and the shrine. My shrine. Worst of all, I remembered trying to go home and falling into the rapids. I shivered even though my clothes and hair were dry. What happened? Why couldn't I go home? It didn't make sense. Before I fell, I'd been close enough to see my house and smell the Lilac bushes towering over the backyard fence.

But I didn't drown. Something or someone caught me and placed me back on the bench. I know it sounds crazy, but that's what happened. Maybe this wasn't a dream or some mean trick after all. Maybe what Billy said was true. I was dead.

But, if I died, lost a day, and missed my audition, why did I feel so alive and so connected to everything around me? I picked a leaf from a branch of a maple tree growing in the center of the boulevard. For a second, my hand merged with the leaf. My palm became the leaf's palm, my life, head, and heart lines blended into the leaf's veins.

"I'm not dead," I called to the tabby cat crossing the street with its tail held high as if it owned the road. I sighed with relief when it blinked its gold eyes at me. "You see me, don't you? I knew it. I'm alive." I blew the cat a kiss. It hissed and slinked under a hydrangea. I kneeled and pushed the branches aside. "Hey, I'm not a spook, you know."

Or am I? I sat on the curb and thought about my grandma's passing, my first experience with death.

She died when I was seven. It was on pancake Saturday, a weekly tradition at my house. Dad would rise early in the morning and make pancakes for everyone. His banging through the drawer of pots and pans would wake me, and I would climb down the stairs to see a huge mess spread across the counter, flour, eggshells, gobs of maple syrup, and Dad looking silly in my mom's floral apron.

When Mom sent me to wake Grandma for breakfast, I found her, lying on her freshly made bed, fully dressed in her Sunday best with her hair done just so and reddish-orange lipstick applied to her lips. Her arms were folded across her chest, and her eyes stared unblinking at the ceiling. Under her breath, she mumbled something that sounded like a prayer.

"Grandma, are you coming down for breakfast?" I asked.

"No, dear." Her voice wobbled like an out-of-tune viola string.

"Aren't you hungry?" I asked.

"Only to see my George."

"He's gone to heaven, Grandma." My grandpa died before I was born, but I had seen pictures of him when he was young, and I must admit he looked hot in his sailor uniform. Grandma said he liked to dance, not just the regular two-step that most guys could manage but swing and jive as well. She said he was the best dancer of all the men in his regiment. A man who could dance was a catch in grandma's day, actually any day. He could sing too. No wonder she was smitten with him. They married when they were only eighteen years old. I wish I had known him.

"I'm waiting for him to come and get me." Her voice was so soft I could barely make out the words.

I sat next to her and held her hand, bony and cold like a turkey wing, all greased and ready for roasting. "You might as well come for breakfast while you're waiting," I said.

Grandma smiled and kissed my hand. "Go get your mom and tell her I need her."

I wiped her reddish-orange kiss from the back of my hand and wished later I'd left it forever. The night after Grandma died, my cat Pixie hissed and growled and puffed like a porcupine. Dad said Pixie could see Grandma coming back for a last visit. I believed him because Grandma forgot to take her purse, and she never left the house without it. I wished I could ask Grandma how she knew it was her time to die. Mom said that Grandma came from a long line of uncanny folks. My parents placed yellow mums on Grandma's grave too.

It worried me because I didn't know how putting grandma in a dark hole and covering her with dirt, and placing a potted yellow mum on her grave would help her get to heaven. Would she have to rise through the ground and push away the pot of mums? When I asked my mother about it, she said it's our spirit, not our bodies, that made the journey to the other side. That didn't make me feel a whole lot better about dying. Separating my spirit from my body at death frightened me. I liked my body. I didn't want to be a spirit that couldn't dance and sing or enjoy chocolate or ride a bike. I'd miss doing my hair and nails. I'd miss falling in love.

In a fit of temper, I knelt and plucked the blossoms off the plant someone left for me by the lamppost and tossed the yellow orbs onto the sidewalk. I wiped tears from my eyes because I knew in my heart my parents placed the yellow mums by the shrine for me.

How could I be dead and still tremble from head to toe? When you die and go to heaven, everything is supposed to be happy, joyful, and peaceful. Isn't it? Besides, if I'm dead, where were the angels and the tunnel of light?

I sat cross-legged on the grass in front of the shrine, opened my bag, and pulled out my kaleidoscope. I pointed it at the lamppost light. "Where are you, God?" I whispered. When no one answered, I placed the kaleidoscope on the mound of cellophane-wrapped flowers. The chilling silence scared me more than seeing my photo propped against the lamppost. What's the point of dying if you don't meet God? Aren't there supposed to be angels? Or a relative like Grandma? Why would God send a stranger to meet me? What did that mean? Oh God! I choked back tears. What if he is a biker from hell? One thing I knew for sure, I was never taking a ride on Billy's Harley.

I listened for his motorcycle and heard nothing except faint scuffing drumming the pavement. Someone ran toward me. In the fading light, I strained to make out the runner's features. As she drew closer, I recognized the bouncing ponytail and the light-footed rhythm. Lucy. She jogged by me. Red curls stuck to the moisture shining on her forehead. She pushed the curls back from her face with the sleeve of my fuchsia sweater. She loved my sweater though the color clashed with her hair.

Lucy dropped her knapsack and knelt by the lamppost. She wiped her eyes. Her crying sounded like a newborn kitten.

"Hey, sis." I crouched beside her and watched her take some things from her knapsack—my things.

"I brought your tap shoes and your favorite CDs. I hope you have a place to play them." She placed my tap shoes beside my picture and the potted mum. She didn't notice I had plucked all the blooms because she pulled the plant toward her nose and sniffed the headless stems. I laughed because it looked so funny.

She pulled a stuffed bear from her knapsack. "And here's Freddie. He misses you. We both miss you." She kissed and squeezed Freddie before placing him by my photograph.

Grandma gave me the stuffed bear on my first birthday. He only had one eye, and his ears were tattered to shreds. He looked at me with his one good eye as if to say, don't leave me. I shuddered to think what would happen to him if she left him by the shrine. He'd get rained on. Or a dog might pee on him or steal him and shake him by the neck and scatter his stuffing all over the neighborhood.

She picked up my picture and looked at it for a long time. "I had so much I wanted to tell you." Her voice broke. "Now, you will never know the truth." She propped the picture against the flowerpot, stood, and stared, like a zombie, all quiet and stiff.

"Truth about what?" I had no idea what she was talking about. I took her hand in mine. It's odd, but a spark, like static electricity, flowed between us. She spun around like maybe she felt it too. She looked straight at me.

"Oh, and I almost forgot. Here's your sweater, just in case you get cold. I'm sorry I took it." She pulled my sweater over her head and placed it around Freddie. A tear slid down her cheek.

There were no kitten sounds this time.

"I want you to keep it. Keep the sweater, Lucy! Just keep it!" It crushed me to see her and not be able to speak to her. She knelt, picked up the kaleidoscope, and aimed it at me.

"Clara?" Her voice trembled. "It's strange, but I can see you inside the kaleidoscope."

I placed my hand on her arm. "Lucy, I'm outside the kaleidoscope, not inside. I'm standing beside you."

This time Lucy saw and heard me. She had that look like when you're suspended at the top of a Double Ferris Wheel and time stretches on forever. You look down at the crowd, cotton candy, gigantic stuffed dogs, and your parents waving to you. You can't smile. You can't laugh. You can't scream. You are way out in front of yourself, and as the Ferris Wheel turns, an instant later, you catch up with yourself. You scream until your throat is raw because it feels so good to finally be able to scream. Lucy's scream sounded raw like that. She dropped the kaleidoscope on the grass in front of the shrine and ran down the street. Without looking back, she disappeared around the corner.

Like a dog chained to a fence, I had two choices, lie down, and wait or fight against the leash. I couldn't let Lucy get away, so I chased her as far as I could.

Chapter Three

Billy sat on his Harley in front of the bus stop and twirled a yellow chrysanthemum between his thumb and forefinger. "Hey babe, are you ready to go now?"

"Not on your life, dude. I'm not going anywhere with you." I was reeling from the sudden and jarring shift back to the bench. Who was he, and why was he the only one I could talk to?

"Ah, babe…" He stuck the yellow blossom behind his ear like a cigarette.

"I'm not your babe. Go away!" I couldn't stop looking at his tattoo, encircling his forearm, a phoenix rising from the flames, typical for a biker.

"Okay, if that's what you want. I'm outta here." His expression, one degree from freezing, chilled me. He kickstarted his hog and shifted into gear.

I stepped off the curb and grabbed the handlebars. "Wait."

I think I surprised him because he raised one eyebrow and

said, "Careful babe, I don't want to run you down."

He revved the engine, and I released the handlebars as if they were hot lava. "Seriously, you'd do that?" I stepped back on the curb.

"Not if you hop on." He patted the seat behind him.

"No freaking way." I crossed my arms. "I have questions."

Billy turned off the engine. "I'm listening."

"If I'm dead, then why can't I remember how I died?"

"You will in time."

"Why not now?"

"Because it's the reason you're stuck."

"Tell me how I died, and I'll be unstuck."

"It doesn't work like that. Anyway, you wouldn't believe me if I told you."

He might be right about that. I didn't trust the guy, but since he was the only one around, I had to ask, "How long can I stay here?"

"As long as you want to." He sighed. "But let's face it, babe, eternity is a long time to be hanging around a bus stop."

"Why can't I leave the bus stop? I get so far, and I end up back here."

"That's because you're between life and death, and it's hard to get around if you don't know what you're doing, which you don't. You're like a baby learning to walk. Once you crossover, it's a piece of cake."

"And if I don't want to crossover?"

"Well, babe, you'd better hug that lamppost cause you're in a place that's neither physical nor non-physical, and if you lose your way, well, you just might end up swimming in the void." He lifted his leg over the seat and leaned against his hog with one boot resting against the curb.

"You're just trying to scare me."

"You think?" His freaking-weird eyes froze me.

"But I don't get it. The road to heaven can't be this hard, can it?"

"For some, it is."

I thought about my mom and dad and how sad they would be to lose me. My dad never got over the death of his brother, who died in a car crash, and it took months to get Mom to smile after Grandma died. "So, why are you here and not my grandma? I've never met you."

"She's waiting for you, but she's not a Light-Keeper."

"A what?"

"Like a lighthouse. A guiding light for ships lost in the fog. Someone who lights the way to the other side. I enjoy bringing people home. It's my talent, and I'm proud to say I'm good at it."

I rolled my eyes. "So modest." Seriously, did this guy have a big ego or what?

He spit on his palm, slicked back his hair, and glanced at himself in his side mirror. I wasn't getting this guy. Was he teasing me or just being a badass? "So, you're a ferryman of sorts, like Charon in Greek mythology."

"You could say that."

"Except you don't row a boat. You ride a Harley."

"Well, I need to keep up with the times. There aren't many people asking to cross by boat these days. If you want, we could go now. I think you're ready." He took the yellow mum from behind his ear and tossed it into the air. A lighted pathway spiraled before me.

A pull, or rather a deep yearning to move forward through the light, overwhelmed me. I backed up, sat, and gripped the bench with all my strength. I heard voices from the afterlife calling my name, enticing me to join them. My hands grew numb. I almost let go. I told myself the voices weren't real. They couldn't be. I sang my favorite song in my mind and recited lines from my audition monologue, and when that didn't work, I shouted, "Go away. I don't want to go." The pathway disappeared. Loneliness settled over me. I shivered and hugged myself.

"I guess I was wrong. You're still not ready." He picked up his helmet as if getting ready to leave.

I didn't want him to stay, and I didn't want him to go. I needed more answers, so I asked another question to stall him. "So, Light-Keepers can be wrong?"

"Sometimes."

"Aren't you all-knowing or something?"

"Only about you."

I felt naked. How much did Billy know? Did he know all the little things I did, like the nasty note I wrote in English class about my teacher, who I hated for giving me a bad mark? The whole class got a detention because I didn't confess that I wrote the note. Did he know all my secrets? Did he know how I fought with Lucy and how jealous we were of each other? Did he know when I told lies or that I stole a bubble gum from the store when I was five? Oh God, and did he know about Cindy and me? "You can't know everything about me. That wouldn't be right. It just wouldn't."

"Don't worry, babe, you're not the worst person I've helped cross." Billy looked at me thoughtfully. "Listen, Clara, you need to accept what happened. It's for your own good."

"Don't tell me what I need to do. You don't know what's right for me. You're not my father."

I'd hit a nerve because the phoenix tattoo on his arm came to life and looked as if it would fly right out of the flames. He gave me his best poker face. "I can't make you do anything," he said quietly without taking his eyes off mine. "I'm only your Light-Keeper."

"I don't understand how someone like you could become a Light-Keeper?"

His amber-flecked eyes narrowed. "What do you mean someone like me?"

"A biker." The words caught in my throat. I coughed and turned away from him. The air between us became charged with razor-sharp particles. The uncomfortable silence dragged on without either of us speaking. Now what? I'd ticked off the ferryman. When I couldn't think of anything else to say, I stood and walked over to the shrine.

I picked up the sweater Lucy left under the lamppost and saw a new bouquet of pink daylilies added to the pile with a sympathy card. I opened the card. It was from Isabel, Ashley, and Tina. They visited my shrine during my failed attempt to cross the river near my home. Without bothering to read the sentiment, I ripped it up and scattered the pieces all over the road. I walked back to the bench and sat. "They're such liars. You can't trust them. They pretend to be sorry when they're not." I pulled the sweater over my head.

"You can't trust me either. I pretend to be a Light-Keeper, but really, I'm a biker," Billy said.

Isn't that true, I thought, but I didn't say it out loud. Instead, I said, "It's just you're not what I expected. You know, dressed like a biker and all."

"What did you expect?"

"I don't know. I didn't expect to die."

"Who does? It's always a surprise. Now you need to move forward."

"To where? To what?"

"Many things. I chose to be a Light-Keeper."

"So, you're not just an ordinary spook?" I asked.

"No, we don't send the ordinary spooks to greet the newbies. It can be a rough transition for some people. Like you, you need to be kickstarted."

"What do you mean?"

"For some reason, you won't let go."

"Do you blame me? I'm only sixteen. I want my life back."

"At first, I was angry. I wanted my life back too."

"So, how do you cope? I mean, you're happy now, right?"

"Very happy."

"Don't you miss being here?"

"Yes, I do. It's the small things: the crunch of snow under my boots on a cold day, chilly nights with bonfires smoking, the taste of hot chocolate sweetened with cream and a dollop of honey, the warm spring breeze, the smell of freshly mowed grass, summer's heat and of course riding my Harley with my girl holding on behind me, her breath on my neck."

Billy was an enigma. One moment he scared the hell out of me, and the next, well, kind of sweet, romantic-like. A cool guy if he were still alive. "How can you be happy without all of that? What's on the other side?"

"I can't tell you. I don't want to ruin the surprise, kind of like a birthday present." He smiled, half-serious, half-playing with me.

"I'd like to take a peek before I open it."

"No peeking."

"A squeeze?"

He laughed. "Okay, a little squeeze. I'll tell you this. You're experiencing only a part of what is real. You're much more than you appear to be. I'm more than the Billy you see before you. You'll understand when you return home."

"There's so much I don't understand. For example, if I don't have a physical body, why can I still hear? Reverberation needs matter. I know that from science class."

"Because your body is energy, and energy can respond to other forms of energy. You don't hear the sound; you are the sound."

I couldn't remember learning that in science.

"Your true self is like the many-colored images reflected by the mirrors inside your kaleidoscope. Death is a change of perspective. It's like looking through a different lens."

I picked up the kaleidoscope from the grass where Lucy dropped it, looked through the cylinder, and pointed it at the light coming from the lamppost. Geometric shapes swirled before my eyes. "Why did Lucy see me after looking through the kaleidoscope?"

"It's magic."

I rolled my eyes. "Yeah, but seriously, why? It's a kaleidoscope, not a crystal ball." I sat and placed the kaleidoscope beside me.

"No, but it acts like one. When contacting the dead was all the rage at the turn of the twentieth century, some people found that mirrors, metal, and jewelry, especially crystals, could act as amplifiers. These things absorb the owner's energy, and people who had psychic abilities could tap into the energy absorbed by these items and contact their loved ones. This kaleidoscope is a perfect communication amplifier, and in some ways, it's more powerful than a crystal ball because it has metal, crystals, and mirrors."

I put the kaleidoscope back under the shrine. "I don't believe in that hocus-pocus. Psychics and absorbing people's energy are crazy. I believe in science, like Einstein."

Billy shrugged. "How would you explain it?"

"I don't. Some things in life are a mystery," I said.

"I agree, but doesn't the scientist in you believe there's an answer to all questions? And didn't Einstein say, "The most beautiful experience we can have is the mysterious."

Billy's answers to my questions, answers that made more questions, made my mind spin. Did I exist or not? If I did, who was I? What was I capable of becoming? This kind of science wasn't like anything I learned in school. "I can't stand the way you talk in circles."

"Okay, I won't talk then. Would you like a ride on my hog? I have an extra helmet." He gave me his special smile again: lips together, a slight upward turn at the corners, half-serious, half-joking, and a little scary. Could I trust it?

"Why do you wear a helmet?"

"It completes the look."

Strange how the chrome on his Harley shone in the twilight, and the yellow flames painted on the red gas tank flickered. Part of me wanted to take a ride on his Harley, but my gut said, no, don't do it. Bad idea. This biker-dude-Light-Keeper must be crazy to think I would get on his hog and ride through the pearly gates on a motorcycle from hell. I shook my head no. A ride on Billy's Harley would be a ride of no return. I was sure of that. "I don't feel dead, you know."

"I know. I don't either."

Before I could respond, Mrs. Kelly, the lady who owned the house across the street from the bus stop, came over with a jam jar filled with roses in one hand and a mug of tea in the other. She lives alone and has the most beautiful flower gardens in the neighborhood. Mrs. Kelly placed the roses, all white, by the shrine. She called them the flowers of light.

When she sat beside me, her loneliness settled like a rock against my chest. Every day since her husband died, she sat by the bus stop, drank tea, and chatted to whoever came by to take the bus. Sometimes she would ride the bus all day.

"The roses are in full bloom. They're early this year," she said as if I could hear her, which I could. She sipped her tea, a spicy blend of orange and jasmine, her favorite. The tea was steaming, and oddly, smoke rings rose from the surface. I popped one with my finger, and it landed in her lap. She smoothed her apron, running her hands over crusted flour and red stains.

"You're making the smoke rings, aren't you?" I said to Billy, who leaned against the bus stop with his hands in his pockets. He had a playful grin on his face.

"Oh yes, Billy likes to tease me. Always did, you know. Hello Billy," she said with a child-like wave of her fingers.

My mouth dropped. My heart raced. Funny, because I was the ghost, and I should have startled Mrs. Kelly, not the other way around. "You can see him?"

"Why wouldn't I? He's standing right there in front of me." Mrs. Kelly pursed her lips as if I'd said something stupid.

"You see me too?" I asked.

"Of course, Clara." She patted my hand as if to say, it's alright, dear.

Billy sat beside her, took her other hand, and squeezed it. "Hey, Mrs. Kelly."

"How come you know Billy?" I asked, still trying to process this weird turn of events.

"He used to cut my lawn," she said, leaning into him in a familiar sort of way. "Noisy kid, though. Everything about him was loud, his music, his cars, his motorcycles. I see he's still driving his Harley. I always thought that motorbike would be the death of him, and it was. Would your mother like one strawberry pie or two?"

"Um… Strawberry pie?" How could she talk about Billy dying in one sentence and follow it with strawberry pie?

"The strawberries are plentiful this year, more than I can pick. I've been baking pies all week. Your dad helped me with my taxes last month, and I promised him strawberry pie in return," she said.

"In that case, I'm sure he wouldn't have a problem eating two pies." My mouth watered at the memory of her buttery crust melting in my mouth. I'd never taste it again.

I looked at Billy. "Why can she see us?"

"We are at the place where dreams intersect," Billy said.

"Do you know you're dreaming, Mrs. Kelly?" I said.

"No, dear. You're the dreamer."

"I'm not dreaming, Mrs. Kelly, so you have to be dreaming about me."

"Is that so?" She frowned. "I used to dream of my dear Andy when he passed. There never was a better man than my Andy. He was my best friend, you know."

"I know."

"I was so lonely without him. Now, I get to see him all the time," Mrs. Kelly said.

"Really?" I wondered if her husband was stuck between worlds too.

"Oh yes. It's so wonderful."

"You mean you see him in your dreams."

"Not just in my dreams, honey. Anytime I want."

I picked pastry off her apron's hem. More and more, her memory failed her. When she couldn't remember a word or someone's name, she would drum her fingers on the table until I could guess the word she needed or the phrase she'd forgotten. When I couldn't help her, she would get angry and tell me to leave. The last time I visited her, I found a stainless-steel pot boiling dry on the stove. She didn't have any family to keep an eye on her. I hoped Lucy would go over once and a while and make sure she was okay.

"Mrs. Kelly, do you know I'm dead?"

"Of course, I know. That's why I brought you the flowers of light. It's sad, you being so young and all, but you're in a safe place now."

"No, I'm not Mrs. Kelly. I'm lost. I'm caught in-between. I'm not on earth or in heaven."

"Don't worry. Billy will show you the way." She stood when the bus came around the corner. "Now remember, Lucy, knows."

"Knows what, Mrs. Kelly?"

"About you." Before I could ask her what she meant, she walked over to the bus stop. The doors swished open, and she disappeared into the bus through the front door while a boy stepped out the back door. Peter.

Chapter Four

Peter? Peter, it's me." I placed my hand on his arm to get his attention. To my surprise, he gave me a static shock that left the imprint of his grief running up my arm.

A pale cloak flickering with rays of blue and brown surrounded him as he walked over to the shrine. I wondered if this was his aura. I'd never seen one before. Now, I noticed that everyone and everything radiated light. Peter's light looked sad, and it hurt me to see his sadness following him like a muddy shadow.

He knelt by the shrine and placed a bouquet of pink roses mixed with baby's breath by my picture. Sixteen. One for every year of my life. His reverence scared me.

"Clara," he said, "I…I don't know if you can hear me or not. But if you can, I just want to say…"

I hovered over him. "I can hear you, silly. Get up! Get up!" I wanted to kiss his cheek or brush my fingers over the reddish-blond stubble forming a shadow of a mustache. So cute. So very,

very cute. But I didn't dare touch him, though my heart ached at the thought of never touching him again.

"Oh God, help me. What can I say that will make a difference?" He punched his fist into his hand. "I hate this. I really hate this."

I crouched beside him and brought my lips close to his ear and the gold stud I gave him for his birthday. If I kissed his earlobe, would I feel it soft between my lips one more time? "Peter, I'm right here, right here beside you."

He pulled a glass candle holder and a pink candle from one of his bulging pockets and lit it using a cigarette lighter. I blew the candle out. He tried again and lit a blue candle. With one puff I blew that candle out too. And the next candle and one after that. Peter mumbled curses under his breath. He looked so spooked, like Pixie when she saw my dead grandmother.

Billy walked toward me. *Clara, don't frighten him,* he said without moving his lips. Up until now, Billy kept his distance on the bench by the bus stop. Still, I had no doubt he heard every word I said to Peter.

"Go away," I said without moving my lips. I knew Billy could read minds because he talked inside mine. I wanted him to disappear so I could be alone with Peter. He ignored me and, without granting my request, walked over to Peter, knelt, and placed his hand on Peter's shoulder. "May I help?"

Peter stiffened and turned toward him, his eyes wide with panic.

"Now look who's scaring the crap out of him," I said.

Peter looked like he'd seen a ghost, which of course he had, but why Billy and not me. "I'm here too, Peter. Can't you see me?" I raised my voice and stuck my face close to his. Peter's upper lip glistened with sweat.

"I'm sorry. I didn't mean to startle you," Billy said.

"These candles must be duds. They won't stay lit." Peter's voice sounded lifeless.

Billy picked up the pink candle and handed it to him. "Try again."

With a shaky hand, Peter flicked the lighter and lit the candle. I leaned over and blew on it. Tiny sparks crackled. The flame died, leaving the wick aglow with smoke smoldering in a spiral. With a quick puff, Billy brought the flame back to life. *That one you won't be able to extinguish,* he said, flashing me an impish grin.

Three times I blew on the candle, but the flame grew brighter with each breath. "Why can he see you and not me?"

It's complicated.

"Thanks," Peter said. "I guess you have the magic touch."

"All it needed was a little coaxing." *And some divine intervention,* Billy added for my benefit.

"Did you know Clara?" Peter asked.

"Yes, quite well," Billy said without looking at me.

"That's a lie. I never met you before today," I said.

Billy stood and slid his hand halfway into his jean pocket and spoke inside my mind. *I'm not lying. You should be able to tell that by my aura.*

A soft white light, with shades of lavender and blue, surrounded Billy. It freaked me out to know he could tell by my aura when I lied. Were we all like Pinocchio in the afterlife?

"And you? Did you know her very well?" Billy asked.

Peter stood and backed away from the shrine. "Yeah, kind of. I mean sort of." He stared at his shoes, high-top sneakers with no laces.

"Sort of? What do you mean sort of?" I kicked his runner and got the shock of my life when my foot passed through his sneaker, leaving my toes tingling. I swore he felt me too. He scuffed the toe of his shoe against the pavement as if scraping off dog poo.

Clara. Billy's voice popped into my mind. I held my hands over my ears to block his telepathic voice. It didn't work. I heard him loud and clear. *Don't do that to him.* His eyes leveled on mine.

Peter spied my kaleidoscope, where I left it on top of a heap of cellophane-wrapped bouquets. "Hey, what's this doing here?" He picked it up and held it like a fragile bird.

"I had one of those once," Billy said.

"It's Clara's. I gave it to her yesterday, for her birthday. Imagine dying on your birthday. She must have dropped it when she was waiting for me."

I crossed my arms. "And I'm still waiting."

"So, you gave her a birthday gift, but you only *sort of* knew her?" Billy teased.

"Yeah, pretty much," Peter said.

"What do you mean sort of knew me?" I said. Every bit of me shook with anger. Anger at my death and anger at Peter for not being there for me.

The streetlight flickered, and for an instant, I found myself spinning in a dark place with images of my life flashing before my eyes. I saw faces, some I recognized and some I didn't. I heard bits of conversations, like someone changing radio stations. Sensations of pain, pleasure, sadness, regret, horror, and happiness swept through me all at once. I screamed. The sound vibrated through my body like an electric guitar riff of power chords at a heavy metal concert. I know that sounds dramatic, but well, that's what it felt like.

Billy appeared before me, even though I could still see him standing beside Peter in front of my shrine in the distance. *Watch your thoughts and emotions,* he said. *Being overly dramatic will transport you into the void.*

Overly dramatic? Maybe I was, but getting stuck in the void frightened me more than death.

Focus, he said.

Focus on what? On something, Peter. My anger had taken me away from him when I needed to be closer. Why did he say he only knew me a little when we were tighter than any other couple in the school? Is that what grief does? Was it easier for Peter to pretend I didn't mean anything to him? I closed my eyes and imagined all the things I loved about him: my fingers entwined in his hair, the cedar-green smell of his clothes, and his singing voice, husky in his lower register and choirboy clear in his falsetto. When we were together, I felt safe. Without him, I felt vulnerable. I opened my eyes and saw only one Billy now, the one standing next to Peter.

"I think you must have liked Clara a lot to give her such a nice gift," Billy said.

"Yeah, I guess." Peter rolled the kaleidoscope between his palms. "I hate this. It stinks. It really stinks."

"Sometimes, when things are tough, it helps to focus on something else for a while. Like the kaleidoscope. Each lens gives you a different view."

Peter aimed the kaleidoscope at the lamppost and turned the wheels around and around. While Peter looked through the kaleidoscope, Billy walked over to his Harley. *He'll be able to hear and see you now,* he said to me before swinging his leg over the seat and kick-starting the hog. I didn't think Peter heard Billy rev the motor. He didn't look up or turn around to say goodbye. Instead, he lowered the kaleidoscope and put it into his jacket pocket.

"I wonder what you would say if I told you, I love you," his voice broke into a whisper when he said, love you.

"It depends if you say it or not." I choked back tears.

He spun around. His face turned greenish-white. His eyes were wide, his mouth half-open. "I…I can't be seeing you." I thought he might faint.

"Oh, Peter…" I walked toward him to take him in my arms. He stumbled back. I stepped closer, but he waved me away. "I need to talk to you," I said.

He rubbed his eyes, and when I wouldn't disappear, he cupped his hands over his ears. "Don't talk. I don't want to hear you. Oh god, what's happening to me?"

It hurt to see him back away from me. With every step he took backward, I took one step forward. I couldn't let him get away like I did Lucy. "Please, wait. I'm not imaginary. I'm here with you. I really am."

"No way you are." He turned, and I ran in front of him and laid my hand on his chest. My hand melted right through. We both jumped back. "Shit. Don't touch me." He placed his hand over his heart where I touched him.

"Okay. Don't run away. Stay there. Right there. Please. Please stay with me." I backed up, and so did he. He took a bottle from his jacket pocket, opened it, and took a gulp. Whisky burned my nose.

When Peter's mother died from cancer two years ago, he found it tough to cope. Since his dad had a problem with booze, it wasn't long before Peter started getting into his father's stash. Peter promised me when we started dating that he would stop drinking. He'd been clean for months, so I was surprised to smell alcohol on his breath the night before my death.

After seeing a movie, we were walking home when I suggested

it was faster to take the shortcut through the forest to my house. My parents didn't like us cutting through the woods during the day or night, but sometimes, I would go that way when I was running late.

I must admit, the woods scared me at night, and normally, I wouldn't take the shortcut, but for some reason, when Peter held my hand, nothing scared me. I felt safe and reckless at the same time. Together we were invincible. Together we could be wild.

The moon, one sliver away from full, cast enough light through the trees to brighten the pathway. Still, the landmarks I relied on, a toppled oak leaning onto a neighboring pine and a moss-covered boulder where I saw my first owl, blended into shadows I didn't recognize.

Crickets chirping, and the zing-zing-zing of cicadas filled the air. A feral cat yowled and made me jump out of my skin. I never understood why they made such an awful blood-curdling scream when they mated. A moment later, I heard a screech. Wings brushed the top of my head. I screamed. Peter grabbed me from behind and put his hand over my mouth. "Shhh. It's only a bat. You're going to wake the dead or worse, your parents."

"Only a bat?"

"Sissy," he teased and pulled me toward him for a kiss, gentle and tentative at first, asking with his lips if it was okay. It was, and I kissed him back, my tongue brushing his lips. I tasted something like burnt oak, but I wasn't sure, so I didn't say anything.

The sparkle of fireflies lit up all around us. Peter cupped his hand and caught one, holding it loosely, so the firefly's light escaped between his fingers.

"Can I hold it?" I asked. I folded my hands to make a cage, and he placed the firefly between my palms. Its wings, flapping against my hand, tickled. When I opened my hand, the firefly sparked and flew away.

We wound our way to the water's edge and sat on a rock under a willow tree. The moonlight reflected in ripples off the water. Using the flashlight on his cellphone, Peter carved into the willow's trunk *Clara and Peter forever.* When he turned off the light, we sat under the moonlight and kissed again. That's when I smelled it—whisky. I pushed him away. "You promised me, no more drinking,"

"I'm not drinking again," he snapped and put his hands in his jacket pockets. His anger crushed the forest sounds. The hush unnerved me. I looked over my shoulder and into the dark recess around us. My heart quickened. I heard leaves rustle, a twig snap, and an owl hoot. I no longer felt safe.

"My dad fell asleep watching the game with a whisky flask in his hand," he said. "I took it and finished it off before we went out tonight. It was only a drop. Don't rag on me for a drop."

My stomach did a whirling dervish. It had to be more than a drop for the smell to linger. One drop today, a whole bottle tomorrow. That's the way addictions took control. If Peter started drinking again, it meant he was upset about something. "Tell me, what's wrong?" I rubbed the small of his back.

He stood and walked over to the log we used to cross the river and tested it with his foot. "Have you ever done something you know is wrong, but you can't think of how to make it right?"

"Probably. Why? Like what?"

"Something stupid. Something that hurt someone else, but you didn't mean to." He sat on the log, kicked off his runner, emptied the sand, and slipped it back on.

"I do that to Lucy all the time."

"But she deserves it. Right?"

"Sometimes."

"I mean, have you ever hurt someone who is totally innocent?"

I thought for a moment if I'd ever hurt someone on purpose. "No. I don't think so. Just tell me straight up what happened."

Peter picked a callous on his finger and made it bleed. It would hurt him the next time he played guitar in his band. When I covered his hand with mine to stop him from hurting himself, he shook me off.

"It's nothing," he said. "I shouldn't have mentioned it."

"Nothing? It's more than nothing if it's making you drink again."

He didn't look me in the eyes, though my eyes never left his for a second. His cellphone rang. He looked at the number and held it so I could see who called. Mom. It wouldn't be Dad. He would never have checked on me by calling Peter's cell.

"It's late. I'd better get home, or I'll be grounded tomorrow."

"And we have a date in the morning. Right?" He bit his lip and half-smiled, a little crooked, so endearing. His eyes looked at me, intense, moist, asking if I could forgive him, if I still loved him. I did, more than anything. People slip sometimes, and he needed me to believe in him.

"How could I say no to donuts for breakfast?"

"It's a date then." His hand shook when he took mine and helped me step onto the log. I put my hand on his chest to stop him from following me. "It's okay. I can go the rest of the way. You don't want to miss the last bus."

"If I miss the bus, I'll walk. It's not that far. I can't let you cross the river alone." He tapped the flashlight on his cell to light the way. When I stepped on the log, he held me around the waist and turned me toward him. Water spray, rising from the rapids, cooled our faces. I brushed a strand of damp hair from his cheek and tucked it behind his ear. He ran the back of his hand down my cheek. His fingers touched my lips. We teetered, caught our balance, and held on to one another, laughing until our lips silenced our giggles.

We were foolhardy to try to cross the river in the dark, yet my heart was light with each step. Being in love with Peter made me brave. Nothing bad could happen to us if we were together. He turned off his cellphone, and we lingered for a while, holding each other in the dark. I listened to his breath, heavy and warm against my neck. The owl hooted again. Was it calling to its mate, or was somebody going to die? I shivered and shook the old wives' tale from my mind.

"Cold?" He turned the flashlight on again so I could see him. Shadows crisscrossed his face. "Are you okay?"

"Just thinking," I said.

"About what?"

"You and me forever. Okay?"

He hugged me so tight I could hardly breathe, and I clung to him, not wanting to let go. With a heavy heart, I trudged up the ridge to my house.

Before I opened the gate to our backyard, I turned and watched the light from his flashlight flickering like a firefly through the trees. I could tell he was almost at the log where he could cross the river. Without warning, a gust of wind whipped my hair into my eyes as I squinted to catch another glimpse of his flashlight before it disappeared into the thick underbrush near the river's edge. I thought I heard a splash, or was it the wind rustling through the trees. No, a splash, I was sure of it.

I imagined his body smashed against the rocks and the current stealing him away from me forever. With my heart pounding in my throat, I made my way back to the river. Under my breath, I chanted, *please be okay, please be okay*. When I saw his flashlight bobbing up the incline toward the street, I breathed easier and shouted, "Good Night." He waved his cellphone and disappeared through the trees to the road.

Now, I know why I found it so hard to leave him that night. It wasn't just because I had discovered him drinking again. A part of me must have known it would be our last hug, our last kiss. Whatever happened to Peter caused him to drink again, and now my death made the problem worse.

Peter drained the whiskey bottle and threw it into the bushes.

"You promised," I said.

"Well, some promises are hard to keep, especially when the one you made the promises to is no longer here." He looked over his shoulder. "Hey, where did that guy go?"

"That's Billy. He took off on his Harley. Didn't you hear him?"

Peter looked puzzled. "No. What Harley?"

"He's a ghost."

"Shit." He threw up his arms. "This isn't happening. I swear the guy looked real."

"He is. He's better at being a ghost than I am." I smiled. It was a joke, but his frown told me he wasn't getting it.

"I must be having a mental breakdown."

"That makes two of us. How do you think I'm coping? I'm

scared and so alone. I don't know why this had to happen to me. Am I a bad person or something?"

"My mom was a good person, and she died." He scuffed his sneakers on the pavement.

"I need you to know I'm here."

"You can't be. You're in my imagination because I miss you and I had so much to tell you. And…and I saw the accident. You were injured. Your body was…"

The horror on Peter's face freaked me out. "Oh God, I hope it wasn't gory or anything." I imagined the worst and covered my face with my hands.

"Don't you remember?" he said.

"Not really. At first, I didn't believe I was dead. I had so many questions. Why would I die when I had so many things I still wanted to do? But people die all the time, don't they, and no one knows why. The thing is, I still don't know how."

"You ran in front of the bus," he said like he was reporting the news.

"What? Why would I do that?"

"I don't know. Cindy was with you. Now she's in a coma."

"She was hit too?"

"No. I heard Cindy had an allergic reaction."

"What are you talking about? What was she allergic to?"

"Wasps."

"You're not making any sense. I don't understand how my getting hit by a bus is connected to Cindy being in a coma from wasp stings."

He shook his head. "I don't know, but maybe you ran out onto the street to keep from being stung."

"It's weird, but I saw Isabel, Ashley, and Tina at Al's. They looked like they had bug bites."

"Did they see you?"

"No. I tried to talk to them, but they didn't hear or see me. They must know what happened."

"If they do, they're not talking. No one is," Peter said.

"But you were there, right? You saw it happen?"

"After. I saw you after it happened. I wish I hadn't seen you lying like that on Mrs. Kelly's lawn. C'mon, I don't want to relive this with you, Clara, because the accident flashes through my mind every hour. I can't stand it anymore."

"How do I look now?" I brushed a strand of hair from my cheek. Up until now, I hadn't thought of my injuries or exactly how I had died.

"You don't look hurt, except, oh, I don't know." He cocked his head and studied my face for a moment. My heart skipped a beat when he paused and looked into my eyes. It made me feel alive again to have him giving me his full attention. "Actually, you look kind of angelic."

I smiled. "Really?"

"Really." He smiled back.

"Angelic?" I stepped toward him. I wanted a hug.

He stepped back and turned away. "Yeah."

"You know, I waited and waited for you." I walked over to the bench and slumped down. "After all, if you'd come on time like you promised, I might not be sitting here waiting for you."

"I know." He dropped beside me. I yearned for him to put his arm around me like he used to and pull me onto his lap. But he didn't. He couldn't.

His silence hung between us as impassable as the veil that separated both our worlds. My stomach knotted. I needed an explanation, but he didn't offer me one. My mind was bursting with questions. Why didn't he meet me after school at the bus stop and go with me to my audition? Why was he late? I needed to know. I hugged my sweater, pulled the sleeves over my fingers, and waited for him to say something like he forgot, or that he was sorry, or that he meant to be on time, but something more important came up. Something more important than me. Like Isabel. I just knew it had something to do with her.

At Isabel's last basketball game of the season, we were close to winning the regionals. The score was tied, and Isabel had that fierce look she would get when she tuned everyone out around her.

Watching Isabel dribble down the court, fighting to hang on to the ball, was like watching a pas de deux. She moved like a dancer, her stride rhythmical, her timing dead on. She owned the ball. She owned the game. Unstoppable. With knees bent, she sprung into the air and soared toward the basket. At that moment, time stood still. She looked like she would never come back down as she nudged the ball from her fingertips. The ball hit the rim, turned a half revolution before dropping through the net—the winning shot.

After the game, she bounced up the bleachers and sat beside Peter with her butt touching his. I wished Peter would move his butt closer to mine. I wished I could sit between them. I wished Isabel would go away.

She pulled the elastic from her ponytail and combed her hair back from her forehead with her fingers. How someone could have beads of sweat wetting their forehead and still smell like lavender mystified me. Some people are born cool, and some people must work at it. Isabel was born cool. Secretly, I envied her.

"So…" Isabel gave Peter a nudge with her elbow.

"Yeah, cool game." He scrunched his empty pop can and tossed it under the bleacher. The can bounced against the metal steps five times and fell silent.

"See you later?" She had her hand on his knee.

"For what?" I asked.

Peter looked at Isabel and she at him. He didn't remove her hand. Why? Why didn't he push it away?

"Isabel wants to audition for the band," he said, without looking at me.

"You're a boyband." I seethed inside. Why didn't he ask me to sing in the band if he wanted to include girls? It didn't make sense. I could sing way better than Isabel, and he never asked me to join. Now that I had died, she could have him all to herself. She could sing with him forever. That thought burned inside me.

"It's Isabel. She's the reason you didn't come to meet me. Isn't it?" Dead or not, I could still get angry. Didn't he know how much he hurt me?

"No," he said. "Why would you say that?"

"Because of the band."

"Oh, that. There's no way the guys will want her."

"Then why let her try out?"

"To get her off my back." Peter stood, walked over to the shrine, and lit another candle, a yellow one.

I stood beside him. "You still don't believe I'm here."

"What makes you say that?"

"The candles."

"You're dead, Clara," he said flatly.

I didn't like him saying that. It sounded so final. "I don't need your damn candles because I'm not dead. Any sane person can see that. And what about Einstein?"

"What about him?" He looked confused. He didn't like science as much as I did.

"Energy equals mass times the speed of light squared," I said.

"So, what does that have to do with you?"

"Everything is energy, and energy can't be created or destroyed. Look at me. Do I look dead to you?"

He looked me up and down, not in the way a guy who likes what he sees would look at a girl, taking her in slowly from top to bottom. He looked at me as if examining a dead frog for dissecting. My chest tightened, like when a guy dumps you. Tears stung my eyes.

"I don't know what I'm seeing. It could be you. It could be me imagining you. I told you that already," he said.

"Take my hand." I hoped it would be possible for him to hold it because I longed for him to touch me.

He placed his palm, wide enough for two of my hands against my palm and curled his fingers to interlock mine. I remembered the time he took my hand on our first date when he taught me to ice-skate. I'd fallen hard, knocked the wind out of my lungs, and cracked a rib. He picked me up, pulled off my wet mittens and surrounded my cold hands with his warm ones, and kissed my fingers.

"I can't do this. Can't you see how hard it is for me?" He said as my hand fell through his like a wisp of smoke.

I've lost him. I've lost him forever, I said silently. I can't go back, and I can't go forward.

One candle, now a misshapen pink lump, flickered and went out. Peter picked up the candle holder and dug out the wax. After molding the wax into a ball, he threw it across the street toward Mrs. Kelly's house. That's when I saw Cindy walking through Mrs. Kelly's rose garden. She wore a white hospital gown, and her hair, cut in uneven lengths, stuck out, this way and that. She impaled her hand on a thorn as she drew a white rose toward her. Blood rose between her fingers. "No," I screamed.

"What's wrong?" Peter looked at me as if I had turned into a banshee or something.

"Cindy. Don't you see her?"

"Where?" He looked up and down the street.

"Over there in Mrs. Kelly's garden." I pointed at Cindy.

He looked across the street and shook his head. "She's still in the hospital, Clara."

"No, she's not. Look. She's standing by the rose bush. She pricked her hand on a thorn." I walked to the curb and would have crossed the street to talk to her if I hadn't heard a chime, not a deep resonate tolling of a cathedral bell but a tinkling clatter. I turned around and saw Marty riding toward us on his bike. When I looked back at the rose garden, Cindy was gone.

Chapter Five

Marty dropped his bike by the bench. "Hey, man. I knew I'd find you here. Been here long?"

"A while." Peter glanced at me and mouthed the words, "Should I tell him?"

Marty frowned. "Who are you talking to?"

"No one," Peter said.

I crossed my arms and said, "Now I'm no one?"

"No…um… I didn't mean that." Peter stammered.

"Mean what? You okay?" Marty asked.

"No, not really. You?"

"I feel like shit. Worse than shit. Damn, I wish it were me and not Clara." Marty shuffled over to the shrine and placed a limp bundle of daisies by the lamppost. "I'm sorry the flowers wilted because I took a moment to stop by the hospital to see Cindy before coming here."

"How is she?" Peter asked.

"About the same. It's sad. I feel so helpless." Marty brushed his hand through his hair leaving it spiked on one side. It looked like he hadn't combed it today. That was Marty. Funny, smart, good-natured, generous with his math homework and his lunch, too, if you dared to share it with him. He knelt by the shrine, hung his head, and whispered so only I could hear him. "I guess my secret is safe with you forever." He ran his thumb over a smooth stone, the one a raven gave us the day he told me his secret. It surprised me because he never let on that anything was bothering him. Usually, he was good-natured, easy to make laugh, but he snapped at me over something small last Friday. He acted strange all day. He didn't eat lunch, which never happened, and he skipped physics, his favorite subject. When I asked him what was wrong, he mumbled something about being sick of school, sick of people, and sick of life.

Marty was the most optimistic person I knew, so seeing him down in the dumps like that worried me. I skipped physics and followed him home. He took the shortcut through the forest and over the embankment to the river's edge, where he stepped from rock to rock until he reached a flat-faced boulder in the middle of the rapids. It gave me butterflies to see him sitting there with waves splashing against his perch. The spring runoff was high, and the current fast and dangerous at this time of year. I didn't think he would jump into the rapids or anything. At least I hoped he wouldn't.

I balanced like a trapeze artist with my arms outstretched and traced the same stepping stones Marty had used until I reached him. I sat on the rock beside him and ran my hand over the milky quartz and pyrite embedded in the sun-warmed surface.

It shimmered in the afternoon sunlight. The fresh scent of sweet clover and wildflowers filled the air. I could see why he made this boulder his sanctuary, the perfect place to get away from the world.

"So, what's up?" I shouted above the roaring water gushing over the rocks jutting from the riverbed.

Marty wiped his glasses on his shirt. "Water spray," he said, but I knew the difference between water and tears.

"Hey, life sucks sometimes, doesn't it?" I said.

"Yeah, the pits."

"Anything I can do?"

"Nope." His left eye twitched.

I looked away when I found myself counting the tics. The sunlight reflecting off the water forced me to close my eyes.

"It's my dad." The words flew from his mouth like a cork popping from a champagne bottle, and his secret fizzed out. I'd always had that effect on Marty. It's because I cared about him, and when people care about you, it's easier to let go and speak your mind.

"He…he had an affair. It's over, but…"

"How do you know?"

"I read one of his emails. He'd asked me to help him recover an important file he'd deleted. He's not great with computers. I saw it in the delete file with some other stuff."

He fingered a stone, a nice flat one, excellent for skipping the water's surface. He tossed the stone into the river, where it bounced off a rock and sank into the rapids.

"Does your mom know?"

"Oh god, I hope not. That would kill Mom. It really would."

I followed Marty as he hopped from boulder to boulder until he reached the shore. He squatted by the river's edge and dragged his hand through the water, stirring the silt. I crouched beside him, cupped fish-fry in my hand, and counted them as they bumped against my fingers. "Maybe it's just that seven-year itch thing," I said.

"What seven-year itch thing?"

"You know, like in that old Marilyn Monroe movie, every seven years, men go crazy and start looking to date younger women. My dad is a Marilyn Monroe fan, and I've seen all of her movies."

"Really? Your dad too?" His glasses slid to the bridge of his nose. I pushed them back with my finger. He looked hopeful, like maybe cheating on your wife with a younger woman was the natural order of things.

"Oh, no! My mom would kill him. Besides, she's still pretty." I wished I hadn't said that. Pretty wasn't everything. I mean, it shouldn't be the only thing that keeps people together.

"It's hard to be pretty after six kids. She's done her best for us. Isn't that enough?" He plucked a flat round stone out of the dirt and hurled it into the water. It hit, making a sound like a belly flop.

I watched the water ripple to the shore. "Will you love your wife when she's no longer pretty?"

"Will you love your husband when he's bald and has a pot belly?" he asked.

I don't know how Marty did it, but he could make a joke even when he felt miserable.

"I'm sure everything will work out. Besides, it's over. Right? He chose to stay with your mom."

"No. The other woman dumped him. And there's a kid. My dad's kid." Water lapped over Marty's sandals and wet the hem of his jeans. "No wonder we're so broke. He sends her money."

"That's heavy."

"Don't tell anyone."

The whop, whop, whop of a raven's wings caught us both by surprise. It hovered before us with its wings spread out in a fan. Water droplets shone on its feathers. It squawked and dropped a stone at our feet, then caught an updraft and flew over our heads and into the trees.

I picked up the weather-rounded stone. Pieces of quartz crystal embedded in the pink-colored granite sparkled as I turned it over in my hand.

"Ravens like shiny things," Marty said, taking the stone from my palm. "They're pretty smart too."

"The Raven is the keeper of secrets. I think the stone is a gift for you."

"Cool." Marty rubbed the stone between his thumb and forefinger as if sealing his secret inside it.

How he coped with being the oldest of six kids mystified me. I'd visited his house a few times. It reeked of dinner, diapers, barking dogs, and screaming kids. It made me think I was never going to have children. At least not that many.

Now, I'd never be married or have the chance to have children. I wanted at least one or two. I felt cheated. I'd lost Peter, the opportunity to grow up and be a famous dancer, to have a family, and keep a secret for a best friend.

"Hey, what's that?" Peter asked.

"Just a stone." Marty put the raven's stone back in his pocket. "Clara gave it to me."

"She's here, you know." Peter pointed at me. "Right there, standing beside you."

Strange to have him point at me like I was something that had caught his interest, like a bear or an eagle or a vintage car and not his girl, the one he loved.

"No shit." Marty looked over his shoulder. "Right. Since when did you start seeing ghosts?" Marty dug a stone loose from the ground near the lamppost with his sneaker and picked it up. "What's she doing? Standing around looking all holy or something."

"I swear I'm not giving you crap. She's really here." Peter looked at me helplessly. I shrugged.

"What does she look like?"

Peter's eyes softened as he searched for the right words to describe how I looked now as a ghost. I loved his eyes and slightly lopsided smile. Would I ever get to kiss his lips again?

"She looks like Clara, the same as always," he said.

"You mean, she doesn't look hurt, you know, from the accident?" Marty asked.

"No, she's beautiful."

"You're crazy." Marty wrinkled his nose in disbelief.

"Are you calling me a liar?"

"No, but you're sad, so you think you see her. I want to see her too, but you have to let her go. You do, man, you really do." Marty picked up a pebble and threw it at the bus stop. It hit with a clink and ricocheted onto the street, where it missed hitting the windshield of a passing car. The startled driver honked his horn.

I knelt and picked one flower from Marty's bouquet. "Thanks, Marty. I love daisies."

"Right now, she's holding one of your daisies in her hand," Peter said.

"Ah, c'mon, man. You know she's not here," Marty said, looking sadder by the minute. I wanted to cheer him up, so I brushed the daisy under his chin until the stamens produce a yellow stain. When Marty scratched his chin, I screamed and leaned over and hugged him. Even though my arms fell through his shoulders, I didn't care because I knew he felt the daisy.

"Look, Peter. Marty felt the daisy brush his chin. Ask him?"

"Did you feel Clara rub the daisy under your chin?" Peter asked.

"No…why?"

"You scratched your chin," Peter said.

"It was itchy." Marty brushed his hand over his chin again.

"It was itchy because she tickled you with the daisy," Peter said. "And she gave you a hug." Marty's shoulder blades ripple under his T-shirt as if he were trying to shrug me off.

He squinted and looked my way. He wanted to believe I was here, but the scientist in him took over, and he squatted and counted the daisies. "You must be losing it, and it's not funny. I brought a dozen, and there are still twelve daisies."

"Why are there still twelve daisies when I saw you pick up one?" Peter asked.

"I don't know. I guess my actions don't affect your physical world." I gathered the whole bouquet in my arms. My bouquet looked fresh. Not limp, like the bunch of daisies, Marty placed at my shrine.

"Freaky," Peter said.

"I must have a bouquet of the flower's essence. In death, they are perfect, but in life, they are droopy and spoiled. Like me. The part of me that still lives is healthy, not broken and crushed by the bus."

"What's she saying?" Marty picked up Freddie and pitched him into the air.

I tried to catch him, but he fell through my fingers and into Marty's hand. "Keep him, Marty."

Marty threw Freddie into the air a second time.

"Clara wants you to keep the stuffed bear," Peter said.

"Hey, don't screw with me. That's not funny. You know she's not here. It's your imagination."

"Tell him Freddie is my keeper of secrets like his raven's stone. He'll know what I mean."

"She said Freddie knows all her secrets like your raven's stone."

His eyes opened wide because I was the only one who knew about the keeper of secrets. He rolled Freddie around in his hands. "Did… did she tell you my secret?"

"I swear," Peter said. "I have no idea what she's talking about."

I was relieved when Marty stuffed Freddie in his pocket. "I trusted her. Have you told anyone?"

"No. She didn't tell me your secret."

"That's a bit freaky," Marty said.

"Tell me about it. Don't you think this is freaking me out too?" Peter sat on the bench. I sat beside him.

Marty followed and squatted to sit beside Peter and directly in my lap. Peter grabbed his arm. "Watch where you're sitting."

"Why? Is there bird poop or something?" Marty brushed the seat of his pants.

"No. Clara's sitting there."

"Right." Marty flopped onto the bench, but I stood before he could land in my lap.

"I wonder what it would be like to sit on a ghost or for a ghost to sit on you. I bet it happens all the time. Shall I sit on him and see?" We were always playing jokes on one another. I'd miss that.

"Cool. Do it. I'd love to see what happens if you sit on him," Peter said.

Marty leaped to his feet. "She's going to sit on me?"

"So, what if she does? You don't believe she's here anyway."

"Well, I do, kind of, because of the raven's stone and all but… but if she's here, she knows everything. She knows what happened at the party between you and Isabel."

"Nothing happened." Peter rose and clenched his fists. There was a fire in his eyes. I'd never seen him look so angry. I was afraid he might hit Marty, who stood and puffed out his chest, getting ready to take him on.

Marty could never win a fight with Peter. I had to distract him. "Is that true?"

"No," Peter's aura flickered. Did that mean he lied? "It's complicated," he said. "It's so damn complicated." Peter never screamed at me before. I didn't like it.

I stood between them. "So, that's why you didn't come. I knew it had something to do with Isabel."

"Hey, man," Marty said. "I was there when Isabel came home after you two left the party in her mom's car. She'd been crying. It doesn't take a brain surgeon to put two and two together."

"You don't know nothing." Peter could have reached through me to shove Marty. Instead, he walked around me and punched Marty in the chest.

The blow sent Marty stumbling backward. "I know what I saw, and if you'd met Clara at the bus stop like you promised—"

"Where were you? You're not so innocent in this. You promised to walk Cindy home," Peter said.

"But I couldn't wait for Cindy because of you. Shit, you know that. If the police hadn't come—"

"Shut up, Marty. Shut up." Peter punched him in the arm.

My jaw dropped. "What happened?"

Marty hit him back.

"Stop," I yelled.

Peter shoved him again. "Don't you think I know that? Don't you think I know it's all my fault?"

"It was your fault." Those words stung harder than any punch Marty could have given Peter.

Peter swung and hit Marty in the face, knocking his glasses onto the pavement where one lens popped out. Marty groaned and covered his face with his hands. I cringed to see the metal frames twisted and the nosepiece that had been repaired once before with black electrician's tape bent in two. Marty lowered his hands. No blood, just a knuckled shape bruise on his cheek.

"That was mean. Why did you do that?" I'd never been so pissed with Peter before. He was acting like his dad, screaming and hitting when he was angry.

"I'm sorry," Peter said. He picked up the frames and straightened them as best he could. Marty searched the ground for the glass lens. I pointed to it, a teardrop of light on the grass. Peter picked it up and handed it to him. Marty fumbled with the lens until it popped back into the frame. "Oh God," he moaned. "Oh, God." He sat on the street curb and buried his head in his hands.

I sat beside him. I wanted to put my arm around him but knew that it would comfort me more than him. Marty wasn't the kind of guy to accept a hug easily. We didn't talk for a long while. Marty fidgeted with his glasses, and Peter bounced the tip of his sneaker against the curb. I counted the number of cars driving by us. Five, and each one slowed down to look at the shrine by the lamppost. A woman pushing a baby carriage walked by us. She had a bouquet of flowers and dropped them by the lamppost and then hurried on without looking back. I didn't know her but suspected she was a friend of my mother's. Maybe, one of the ladies from her yoga class.

The lamppost light flickered on. Sundown was pulling the last rays of twilight below the horizon, and soon darkness would fold around us. The barn swallows dived for mosquitoes, in and out of the lamplight. All kinds of birds were chattering in the trees. Crickets lent their voices to the night songs, and from deep within the forest, a bullfrog bellowed out a bassline. The still night air had cooled, and with it came a chilling breeze. I hugged myself inside my sweater.

"Hey, are you okay?" Peter said. "I'm really sorry I hit you. I'm sorry about your glasses."

Marty polished his glasses with his shirttail. When he placed them back on his nose, they leaned to the right. "I need a new pair anyway. I can't see the blackboard from the front row." He stood and with his hands tucked into his pockets, faced Peter.

"You don't sit in the front row." Peter took the glasses off Marty's face, bent the arm a little, and placed the glasses back on Marty's nose. Not quite straight, but better.

"Yeah, right. That's what I mean. What's the point?" Marty bit his thumbnail and ripped it to the nail bed.

Peter rattled the change in his pocket and looked at me. "Why can't he see you?"

"It's the kaleidoscope. It changes the way you see things," I explained. Peter hadn't made the connection. "Give it to him. If the kaleidoscope worked for you and Lucy, it has to work for Marty too."

"Hey, it's rude to be talking to her when I can't hear what you're saying to each other," Marty said. "It's like speaking a different language in front of me or talking on your cellphone when we're at a restaurant. I hate it when people do that. What did she say?"

"She thinks that if you look through the kaleidoscope, you'd be able to see her."

"What? Is it magic or something?"

"It might be." Peter took the kaleidoscope out of his pocket and pointed it at Marty.

Marty pushed the kaleidoscope away from his face and stood. "You're losing it. Cylinders with little glass wheels and mirrors can't make you see the dead."

"You're right. I must be crazy because it doesn't make sense that I can see Clara and not my mom. You know, I thought she'd come back and talk to me. I'd lie awake at night waiting for her to appear in the air over my bed, but she didn't come. Why?" Peter cleared his throat. "Why didn't she come to say goodbye?"

Peter never talked about his mom, but we all watched him struggle after she died. He started skipping school and hanging with the wrong people. I didn't know how to explain why Peter could see me and not his mom. It had to be the kaleidoscope.

Marty placed a hand on Peter's arm. "Hey, man. It's probably for the best. There's a reason why dead people are invisible." When Peter stepped away, Marty made a fist and shoved it into his pocket.

"And why's that?" Peter asked.

"Because they have to move on," Marty said. "Both of you do. If you can really see her, maybe you should tell her to leave."

My throat tightened. "Do you want me to go?" I whispered.

"Maybe you should," he said.

My eyes blurred. "Please, Peter, let Marty look through the kaleidoscope. If he sees me, you'll know you're not crazy."

Peter handed the kaleidoscope to Marty. "At least take a look. Do it for me. Do it for Clara. If it worked for me, it might work for you."

Marty examined the three-sided barrel made of mirrors and wheels crafted of stained glass, beads, and metal buttons welded together. "Cool Kaleidoscope. I've never seen one like this before."

"I gave it to Clara. She had it with her when she died. Try pointing it at the light from the streetlamp," Peter suggested.

While twirling the kaleidoscope's wheels, Marty walked around the lamppost. "Wow. You're right. It's not a normal kaleidoscope. It's like looking through to another world. I want one of these. Where did you get it?"

"From a guy I met downtown." Peter's face paled. "You know, he looked a lot like Billy. I thought I recognized that dude. Only he wasn't dressed like a biker."

"Who's Billy?" Marty knelt on one knee and pointed the kaleidoscope at a candle.

"A busker. He was playing the clarinet, blues, and jazz. Really smooth. He had the kaleidoscope propped against his clarinet case. I asked him about the kaleidoscope, and he let me have it for ten bucks."

"Billy? You mean the biker?" I asked.

Marty heard me and whipped around and gasped. His eyes bulged wider than a bullfrog. I thought he'd pee his pants.

"Holy shit!" He took a deep breath and held it.

"I'm not a ghost, silly. Well, not that kind of ghost."

"But…" He exhaled sharply and wiped the sweat beading across his upper lip.

"It's me. I'm really here. You haven't died and gone to heaven." I hoped my attempt at humor would calm him, but he didn't even smile.

"Shit... I'm not believing this." Marty backed away, dropped the kaleidoscope, and ran to his bike, and hopped on. He caught his shoelace in the chain and had to stop to pull it free, which he did by yanking it until it broke.

"Stop. Wait a second. She's not going to haunt you. Right, Clara?" Peter grabbed the handlebars before Marty could pedal away. "It's okay. I see her too."

"What's she doing here? She should be in heaven where she belongs. Let's get out of here."

"I can't leave her, Marty." Peter looked at me helplessly. "If we both can see her, it means we're not crazy. It means she's here all alone."

Marty looked over his shoulder at me. "She's a ghost, not a lost kitten. You want her to haunt you for the rest of your life? Hurry. Hop on."

"I'm sorry, Clara," Peter said. "Forgive me. Seeing you is messing with my head. I...I need time." Peter hitched a ride on Marty's wheel pegs. Marty took off as fast as he could with the extra weight.

I ran after them and yelled, "I promise, guys, I won't haunt you. Please wait." I pushed as hard as I could against the restraints pulling me back to the bus stop. The further I ran, the dizzier I became. I used all my will to keep going, and my determination paid off. I felt a snap, and my world, such as it was between life and death, disappeared. I'd broken the bond that held me to the bus stop, only to fall into the abyss from my dream.

Chapter Six

Black. Blacker than black. Words could not describe this place—that wasn't a place—where I found myself dangling without form. I couldn't hear my screams or feel my hands and feet, yet I still had my mind, and I have to say, being alone with my thoughts terrified me.

Was this the void, the place of nothingness manifested? If so, was I stuck here forever? Panic gripped me. I'd never felt so terrified and vulnerable. I had to find a way to escape before this place of unmaking absorbed my sense of self, and I too became nothing.

I needed help, and the only one who could help me was Billy, my Light-Keeper. How on earth or heaven would Billy be able to find me, a mere thought, in this empty place? He wouldn't be able to see me because I was formless, and he wouldn't be able to hear me because I couldn't make a sound. Or could I? What did he say? You become the sound. In my mind, I called his name over and over and as loud as possible. I waited and waited for an answer, but none came.

Billy said to focus. Focus on what? There was nothing in this empty place to focus on except my memories. So that's what I did. I thought of Mom and Dad and Lucy and how much I loved them and how much they loved me. I held the thought of their love in my mind. It worked. I accelerated, not up or down or sideways but inward. I screamed and screamed and screamed.

I awoke screaming face down on something soft—my bed. I squealed, kissed my pillow, and threw the covers aside. Through my open window, I could see the moon in its first-quarter over the chestnut tree. I was alive. I looked around at the posters covering my walls, my favorite rock band, my favorite dancers, Nijinsky, Nureyev, Fontaine, Baryshnikov, Karen Kane, Derek Hough, and all my dance awards cluttering the dusty shelf by my desk. Ballet shoes, worn to shreds, lay in a heap in the corner of my room. What a dream. What a terrible, terrible dream. I crawled out of bed. My room smelled like home, a mixture of candles, incense, and perfume. I scooped my dance shoes off the floor and held them to my nose, relishing the smell of leather and sweat. Giddy with happiness, I opened my bedroom door. Voices argued downstairs. I walked to the landing and looked over the railing.

Lucy stood on the bottom stair. "Nothing's going to happen to me," she said. "You're smothering me with your fear. I can't live as if the world is a dangerous place."

"It is a dangerous place. You've seen the news." Mom sounded tired. I strained to see her over the railing, but she was standing in the kitchen.

"I just want to see a movie with Tommy," Lucy said. "I'll phone you when I get there. I'll phone you when I leave the theatre. Okay?"

"I don't want you going to a late showing. You won't be out

of the theatre until eleven. I said no, and I mean it." Mom's voice rose in pitch, sharp and shrill.

"Why? It's Saturday. I don't have school tomorrow." Lucy could still whine like a spoiled kid when she didn't get her way. It usually worked for her but not today.

"No," Mom said. "And that's the end of it. Now take these clothes. I washed them for you." Mom stepped onto the bottom stair with a bundle of folded clothes in her arms.

"I don't want them," Lucy said. "I told you before. I don't want Clara's hand-me-downs."

"It's a shame to give such nice clothes away. I know Clara would want you to have them," Mom said.

"No, I wouldn't…" I began and stopped myself. The words caught in the back of my throat. Disappointment crushed my short-lived happiness. Somehow, I'd traveled beyond the barrier by the bus stop, through the void, and arrived home. Dead. Still dead.

"Ever since Clara left us, you've been suffocating me. You have to let me live my life." Lucy brushed by me as she ran up the stairs. I know she felt something because she stopped and glanced in my direction.

"Lucy," I whispered.

She either ignored me or didn't hear me. I almost spoke to her again, but Mom interrupted the moment and called to her, so she continued her sprint up the stairs. Her footsteps thumped against the hardwood floor. Her bedroom door slammed shut.

Mom trudged up the stairs, flip-flopping in her slippers. I followed her into my bedroom, where she placed my freshly laundered clothes on top of my dresser. I watched her put my neatly folded clothes away: my favorite nightgown, my hoodie with our school crest, my silk lavender shirt, and low-cut jeans. All the things Lucy used to like to steal. When Mom finished tucking everything into the drawers, she opened the bottom drawer and took out my diary, leather-bound and etched with moons and stars. It oozed with all my private thoughts. If I could have snatched the diary out of her hand, I would have.

When I sat beside her on the bed, she looked right at me. "I'm here, Mom. Can you see or hear me?"

Mom opened the diary, and a picture fell into her lap. Julian, Ashley's older brother. Five years ago, when Ashley's parents divorced, he moved in with his dad while Ashley stayed with her mother. When he was young, he was a pimply boy with a brush cut and monkey ears. At sixteen, Julian was a professional actor and cool in that heartthrob sort of way. He had smoking hot eyes, a layered hairstyle covering his big ears and hips like a Latin dancer. Just plain yummy.

He came to see Ashley perform at the award ceremony, where my photo was taken wearing the slinky black dress. I didn't want to get caught gawking at him like some of the other girls, but I did sneak a look while he was standing in the concession line. I didn't expect to find him staring at me. I looked away quickly. Surely, he wasn't interested in me. I looked again and held my breath while my stomach turned somersaults. I'd never had a guy look at me like that, a cute guy that is, a guy that everyone wanted.

For days, I couldn't stop thinking about him. I kept hearing his voice whispering in my ear. "Loved your performance. Your dance solo was the best. You looked great up there. Have you ever considered getting an agent?"

Three days later, Julian called. Lucy answered the phone.

When she yelled, "It's a boy! It's a boy!" I wrestled the phone out of her hand and hid in the laundry room. I smiled when he asked me for a date in his falsetto voice. He cleared his throat and asked again in his normal baritone range.

So, I made him feel as nervous as he made me, which empowered me to say yes. After we said good-bye, I stayed for ten minutes in the laundry room and folded and counted all the clothes piled on the dryer: five men's t-shirts, seven pairs of socks, three without mates; twelve pairs of underwear, three white, five with flowers, two black, one denim blue and one thong. A thong. Too small to be Mom's. It had to be Lucy's. What did Mom think when she found the thong in the dirty laundry? I hope she didn't think the thong belonged to me.

"Who was that?" Mom looked up from her crossword when I tiptoed from the laundry room.

"Oh, no one. Just a guy from school who wants to borrow my science notes. He had that terrible barfing flu Lucy had last week. Poor guy. He hurled all over his science partner. The entire classroom stunk so bad, and I thought I'd lose my tuna salad sandwich right in the middle of dissecting a cow's eye."

I winced after I said it. My lies were getting more elaborate, and I may have gone too far with this one. It didn't ring true like some of my other fibs, but I had to lie to keep from hurting my parents. Mom would disapprove of my date because Julian was sixteen going on seventeen, and I was fourteen going on fifteen. Not a big difference in my mind but to my parents, a generation gap.

Mom knew I was hiding something. The folded laundry gave me away. I never folded my clothes because if I did, I'd have to count them. Everyone has at least one strange quirk, and mine is counting. I count when I'm stressed. She asked me to come back downstairs and talk to her after I finished putting the clothes away. I mumbled I would and climbed twelve stairs to my bedroom. After I dumped the clean clothes, everyone's clean clothes, into a heap on my bed, I buried my head in my pillow and screamed.

How would I manage to get through the next day? If only a day didn't have twenty-four hours because now, I'd have to count every hour, every minute, and every second until my date. That was 86,400 seconds.

And, what if he tried to kiss me? I'd pictured it a thousand times, how to turn my head, how to place my lips, pressed together or slightly parted. And what do I do with my hands? My tongue? I'd have to remember not to eat anything with garlic for lunch.

Julian waited for me after my last class. He looked like a model in his black jeans, rock-band t-shirt, and leather jacket flung over his shoulder.

"Sweet." With heavy-lidded eyes, he checked me out from top to bottom. My stomach flopped again and again.

I'd refreshed my makeup before my class and put on a circle skirt with black leggings and a cute sleeveless V-neck ruffled blouse. He pressed his hand into mine and twirled me around so he could admire my short skirt flaring above my knees. I'd never held a guy's hand before. It felt awkward and nice at the same time. His boots clicked on the hallway floors, a drumbeat in sync with my heart. More than one head turned as we walked down the hall. When I teetered on my heels, he caught me around the waist. I talk a lot when I'm nervous, but at that moment, I couldn't think of a single thing to say. I mean out loud.

He took me for Mexican food and later to the Playhouse

Theatre for an evening of improv. I enjoyed the enchiladas and the theatre sports, but after he drove me home and he walked me up the sidewalk to the front step, he stopped under our chestnut tree, took my hand, and drew me toward him. He twirled a strand of my hair around his finger before brushing my hair back from my face. It was the moment I dreamed of. The kiss. I don't know why, but I panicked. A dizzy not-in–my-body feeling came over me when he planted his mouth on my dry, thin lips. The magical moment I imagined turned out to be a letdown. I felt nothing but his tongue on my teeth and his lips sucking on mine like a toilet plunger. When he grabbed my boobs, it hurt, so I pushed him away. It was that time of the month, and just walking down the stairs was excruciating. His head clunked against the tree trunk knocking a couple of chestnuts on the ground.

"I guess I caught you by surprise." He forced a smile and rubbed his head.

"Yeah, a little." I thought, if I died now, I wouldn't have to wake up tomorrow and remember the pained look on his face and how he stumbled over his goodbyes to me.

He didn't call me after that kiss. I was devastated. I couldn't tell anyone about my night out with Julian, or they would think there was something wrong with me because I couldn't keep a guy as cute as him. But my sister Lucy knew. It was one of those times we connected heart to heart like sisters should.

While I was lathering my face, she barged into the bathroom and sat on the edge of the tub, and said, "It's stuck on your lips forever. You'll never be able to wipe it off."

"What are you talking about?"

"You know." She puckered her lips.

"I hate you," I said, each word punctuated by soap bubbles. "You were spying on me." I warmed a faced cloth, wiped away the lather, and looked in the mirror, and groaned.

"You still see it, don't you?" Lucy covered her mouth to hide her smile.

"Shut up."

"It's not that you look different after your first kiss. It's you feel different, and when you feel different inside, it shows outside."

"What do you know about kissing?" I asked.

"It's fun. I like it."

"You and Tommy?" I was shocked. Lucy was only thirteen, and she had already had her first kiss.

"Yeah, who else would I kiss?" she said.

She'd been dating Tommy all year and never once brought him home. I should have known they were serious because every time I saw them together, they were holding hands.

"He's good. Really good. He taught me…"

"Don't tell me." I put my hand over her mouth. "I don't want to know."

She pushed my hand away and laughed. I felt miserable. When it came to guys, I was Lucy's baby sister. "How much did you see?"

"Everything. I was walking home with Janie when we saw you under the chestnut tree with Julian. We ducked behind a car to watch." She giggled.

I threw my towel in a heap by the toilet, skipped brushing my teeth, and stormed out of the bathroom. I was beside myself with worry. It wasn't just Lucy who saw me but that blabbermouth Janie. Now the whole neighborhood, the whole school would know. I might as well die. My life was ruined. Who would ask me on a date now?

Later, Lucy crawled into bed with me. She smelled like her favorite soap, Lilly of the Valley. "I brought you something."

"What?"

"It's a surprise. Hold out your hand." The light shining in from the street cast a shadow on her wicked smile.

"I'm not in the mood for any of your tricks Lucy. Go away." I leaned back on my pillow and pulled my quilt over my head.

She pulled the covers aside and straddled my legs, pinning me to the bed. "It's not a trick."

"Get off me." I tickled her until she rolled to the side. I sat up. "I don't want whatever it is you have. Now get out."

"You don't know what it is."

"I don't care what it is."

"Oh, c'mon, it'll cheer you up."

"Go away." The only thing that would cheer me up right now was a permanent muzzle on chatterbox Janie and maybe some— chocolate. "Is it edible?"

"I guess you could eat it if you're hungry. Hold out your hand."

There would be no peace until I let Lucy play out her prank. I held out my hand, expecting cooked spaghetti or something slimy like defrosted spinach. It took a moment for me to recognize what Lucy dropped into my palm. Two smooth chestnuts.

"A souvenir." Lucy laughed so hard she doubled over into the fetal position. "You looked like you'd eaten a lemon when he kissed you. And…and his eyes almost popped out when you pushed him into the tree. He deserved it for feeling you up. What a jerk."

Lucy made me laugh at myself, and the next morning the residue of my first kiss washed away with soap and water. Now

I know the difference between having a crush on a guy and really loving him. It makes kisses sweeter when you fall in love for real like I did with Peter.

"Clara," Mom said. "I didn't know about Julian." She placed Julian's picture back in the diary and turned the page. My first kiss with Peter would not happen for many months. She would read my story eventually and be happy for me. Happy that I found love, sad that I lost the love of my life so young. She surprised me when she flipped through the pages. She was looking for something. Something about Peter, and she found it written in all its glorious detail. My private moment.

Don't read it, Mom," I said. "That memory is for me. Let me have that one to myself." She closed the diary and placed it underneath the clothes in the dresser drawer. I sighed with relief. One day, she might read it but not now, not while I watched.

I followed Mom across the hall to Lucy's room. She knocked, and when Lucy didn't answer, Mom opened the door and walked in.

I looked around at her insanely organized bedroom. Lucy always made her bed in the morning, shelved her books in alphabetical order in her bookshelf, and never placed posters or pictures on her walls. She didn't have any dolls or stuffed animals to clutter her space as she never wanted or played with toys. She lived like a monk, and in some ways, she was. Sports, especially running, was her religion. Her shrine was the treadmill that filled half her bedroom.

The wind blew through the open window and ruffled the curtains. Lucy must have crawled out the window and onto the roof. The drop to the ground wouldn't worry her. She had done it many times before.

Mom sat on Lucy's bed and burst into tears. I longed to hug

her like she used to comfort me. Where was Dad? He should be holding her and telling her he loved her and that they would get through this together. How quickly my thoughts brought me to him in the basement.

I found Dad framing in the playroom he promised to build for Lucy and me. Mom planned it to become a guest room when we outgrew it. She nagged him every weekend to get it done, but he never found the time to finish it until now.

Dad hunched over a piece of lumber. He had a pencil in his mouth and a measuring tape in his hand. I calculated the 2 by 4's length before Dad had a chance to pull the measuring tape from the case. I told him the size, and he repeated what I told him before he measured the wood. Three times we did this together. Each time the number was the exact measurement. Too many times to be a coincidence. I don't know why I had this talent. It was the same with math. When Dad balanced books for his clients, I would calculate the sum of a column and give him the figure before he could total it with his calculator.

Dad threw down his tape measure. "Baby?"

"I love you, Dad." He heard me because I saw tears in his eyes but, when Mom came down the basement stairs, he looked away and wiped his eyes on his sleeve. Mom leaned against the 2 by 4 framing the doorway and watched Dad use the skill-saw to trim another stud. "It's coming along," she said over the high-pitched squeal cutting a chasm between them.

Dad picked up the 2 by 4 and set it in place. "Can you hold it?"

Mom held the stud while Dad picked up his nail gun. "Lucy's gone," she said. "She crawled out her bedroom window to see that boy. She won't listen to me. I'm tired of it. I'm tired of worrying about her. Ever since Clara left us—"

Dad shot a round of nails into the stud. More nails than it needed. "I'll take the car and look for her. Do you want to come?"

"I'm pretty tired. Do you need me?" Mom said.

He put the nail gun down and sat on his workbench. "I guess not." He stood and picked up another piece of lumber—cracked on one end. He tossed it back on the woodpile. He had a faraway look in his eyes. He needed to hold someone. He needed to hold me.

"Don't worry, Dad. I'll find her," I said.

Now that I had figured out how to free myself from the boundaries that kept me near my shrine, I learned very quickly that thought alone, if focused, could get me where I wanted to go.

Chapter Seven

Some people spend their lives taking shortcuts and never doing anything full out. Not Lucy. Halfway is not in her vocabulary. She's an all-or-nothing kind of girl and fearless in a reckless sort of way. Sometimes she leaves me breathless with her choices. When it comes to rides at the fair, the scarier, the better. Extreme sports like zip-lining, windsurfing, and rock climbing suit her temperament more than yoga or dancing. In all things, she is a thrill-seeker. Not me. I don't get a rush from trying to scale a rock face with nothing but a rope to keep me from plunging to my death. In everything, except my dancing, I play it safe. I guess that's why I've never been able to get into the altered state of mind that Lucy reaches with her long-distance running.

Running is her passion, and no one can beat her at our school. She breaks every school record locally and nationally. I'm awed by her stamina. When everyone else is falling by the wayside, she slips into "the zone," the euphoric feeling of being outside the body, where she feels like she's soaring.

Mom would have a conniption fit if she knew Lucy made a habit of running around the school track this late at night. Floodlights illuminating the field allowed me to see Lucy jogging around the track. She looked so vulnerable, so small, so alone. I waited until she came abreast of me and fell into step beside her, and matched her stride. When I was flesh and bone, I would never have been able to maintain the brisk pace, but in my light body, it was easy to keep up with her.

I could tell Lucy was in "the zone" because her eyes were half-closed, her pace easy, and her breathing measured. Damp curls bounced against her neck. I listened to her breath, a rhythmic hissing interspersed with the occasional sentence, "Why did you have to freaking die? You're crazy if you think I'm going to wear your stupid clothes. All Mom and Dad do is fight about you. They can't get over it. You've ruined their life, and you've stolen mine. They're lost in their grief, and they blame me."

"How could they blame you? It wasn't your fault. It was an accident." I hoped she could still hear and see me. Her pace quickened. I matched it.

"You don't know what it's like. You don't know how hard it is. I hate how your death changed everything." She paused, bent over, and pulled up her sock. The night air pulsated with the sound of her breath, heavy and sad.

"Lucy," I said. "Can you see me?"

"No, but I can hear you." Her voice quivered. She brushed a damp curl from her eyes, no make-up, prettier than ever. "Where are you?"

"I'm beside you."

She pawed the air passing her hands through mine. The kaleidoscope's effect must have been temporary. She could hear me but not see me.

"I can't do this, Clara. It's too hard. Please go." She sprinted across the field toward Tommy, who waited for her in the shadows near the school's entrance.

I followed, keeping in step beside her. "Don't do this to Mom," I said. "You're hurting her."

"You're one to talk. No one has hurt Mom more than you. Don't you know how you've changed our lives? My life?"

"Two days is not your whole life."

"More like five months."

"What?" I stopped running, not to catch my breath but to absorb what she said.

How long did I stay suspended in that void? What happened to time? Five months had passed since I died. No wonder the kaleidoscope's effect had faded. What about my funeral? I'd missed that too. I thought of the shrine and Peter and Marty. Would the shrine still be there if I went back to the lamppost? Would I have already been forgotten? Where was Billy? Could he find me five months into the future?

Lucy ran into Tommy's arms.

"Who were you talking to?" He said, dropping a butt and squishing it into the tarmac with his sneaker. The smell of pot lingered in the air.

"No one. Let's go, okay?" She linked her arm into his and walked right by me. "Do you have some more of that?"

He lit a joint and handed it to her. To my surprise, she took a puff.

"Lucy, you'll never get to the Olympics with drugs in your

bloodstream. What happened to your dream?" She heard me because she took another drag and blew the smoke in the direction of my voice. I watched her leave the school grounds with her arms around Tommy.

I turned away with a lump in my throat and walked across the sports field. I wasn't ready to go back to the bus stop, so I decided to go by Cindy's home. When I was alive, I usually ran, not walked through her neighborhood. Tonight, I didn't care. No one could see me. I didn't have to worry about hoodlums in slow-moving cars or drunks following me down the street. For the first time, I could get a good look at the houses. Some were tended with lawns and gardens, while others looked rundown with knee-high weeds. Kids abandoned bikes on driveways, chalked hopscotch on the sidewalk, built makeshift forts in the backyards.

I walked by a pickup truck parked on someone's lawn. The fogged windows kept me from seeing inside. I crossed the street and took a shortcut through a neighbor's unkempt yard. I heard a baby crying. A man yelled at the baby to shut up. A woman cursed the man. The baby screamed louder. From out of nowhere, a growl startled me. I spun at the same moment a mastiff snapped at me. The chain around its throat choked it before it could reach me. I didn't want to take a chance the dog could bite. After all, it could see me, so I gave it a wide berth and continued.

Cindy's house, a two-bedroom rancher with peeling gray paint, was the last house at the end of the street. Yellowed plastic, taped over the windows, flapped in the breeze. One of Cindy's birdfeeders lay upside down in the corner of the porch. Birdseed pebbled the sun-bleached deck. Runaway newspapers, windblown from the pile at the doorway, clung to the siding and around the deck rails. A man's undershirt fluttered on the clothesline.

I'd visited Cindy's house a month ago. One month? No, it must be six months now. My math teacher asked me to drop off her homework on my way home from school. She'd been absent for at least a week, home with the flu, they said. When I talked to her, she told me she hadn't been sick at all. Something else kept her away from school, something nasty.

Cindy didn't have many friends at school. I don't know why she didn't fit in or why we singled her out to be the one. Was it because she was shy? Was it because her pants were too short, and she always smelled like cigarettes?

She wasn't ugly, but she wasn't model-pretty either. Shoulder-length brown hair framed her oval face, high cheekbones, and hangdog eyes. One of her nicknames was toothpick because of her flamingo-thin legs.

Some kids, like Cindy, struggled to fit in at school. The week before she stopped coming to classes, someone dented her locker door so that you could get your arm through the opening at the top. In art class, she discovered her unfinished sculpture of a heron smashed to pieces. By the end of the week, when we had to choose partners for a science project, she was a nervous wreck. Most of the time, Cindy partnered with Marty for group science projects. Everyone wanted to be Marty's partner because that would guarantee a perfect mark. No one wanted to be Cindy's partner so Marty, would always choose her first. Sometimes students tried to come between them, and usually, Marty would remain faithful to Cindy. That is until Ashley asked Marty to be her partner.

Ashley needed to improve her marks, but that wasn't the real reason she chose Marty to be her partner. She wanted to make

Cindy's life more miserable than it already was. You see, Cindy had an enormous crush on Marty, but Marty had an enormous crush on Ashley. Cindy didn't have a chance competing against Ashley. She was the one girl that Marty would choose over Cindy. I'd never seen Cindy so upset. She wouldn't talk to me or join my group. She said she wanted to work alone, but Cindy never completed the project because she stopped coming to classes.

A tall thin woman met me at the door and invited me in. I introduced myself, and she told me her name, Lana. Cindy's mother surprised me because I expected to see her wearing jeans or sweatpants, not a form-fitted black dress with high heels. Her low-cut dress showed enough cleavage to make me blush. It also allowed me to see the edge of a tattoo, a bird's wing on her breast. Lana's make-up enhanced her big eyes and high cheekbones. Her hair, flat-ironed smooth, fell to her shoulders. I could see where Cindy had inherited her pretty face. Lana looked about the same age as my mother; only, my mom would never wear a dress or blouse with a neckline showing so much cleavage.

The house smelled smoky, and I stifled a cough as I followed Lana into the kitchen. Cindy was sitting in the breakfast nook.

"Clara brought your homework," Lana said before submerging her hands in the kitchen sink to finish washing the dishes.

Cindy dog-eared a book and pushed it to the side. I glanced at the title, a book about endangered birds.

"Hi." I stood in the middle of the kitchen and waited for her to acknowledge me, but she didn't look up or say hello. She took a burning cigarette from the ashtray and stirred the ashes with it. When Lana wasn't looking, she snuck a drag.

"Cindy, don't be so rude. Offer Clara a glass of juice or

something. A coke?" Lana said.

"No, thank you." The kitchen didn't look clean, and seriously, I didn't want to catch anything.

When Lana reached for her cigarette, Cindy quickly moved her hand away from the ashtray but not fast enough. Lana snatched the cigarette out of Cindy's hand and waved the burning wand at her. "I'd better not catch you smoking this crap, Cindy. I bet Clara doesn't smoke."

I shook my head. "No, I tried it once but never liked it."

Cindy rolled her eyes and gave me a fleeting what a sis look.

"Good, because it's a dirty habit." Lana took a long drag and turned back to washing the dishes.

I sat opposite Cindy in the nook, on top of a crack in the leatherette upholstery. Stuffing bulged from under the curled duct tape used to mend the tear. It kept pinching my thighs. I squirmed to find a comfortable spot and wished I'd worn long pants instead of shorts.

"Math." I pushed her homework toward her.

"I hate math." She pushed it back and wrinkled her nose.

Lana wrung out the dishrag and hung it over the water faucet. "Well, you'd better start paying attention to your schoolwork, or you'll be working two-bit jobs for the rest of your life."

"I could help you," I offered. "Math is my best subject."

Cindy stirred the butts in the ashtray with her finger. "Yeah, I know. You have some freakish talent with numbers."

"So, I heard you have a freakish talent with art," I said.

"Who told you that?"

"No one. I've seen your stuff."

"Really?" For the first time since I walked into the kitchen, she looked at me. I'd never notice until now that her eyes were a striking violet shade.

"What's wrong with you anyway?" I asked. "You don't look sick."

A cupboard door banged. "Look at the mess of her hair." Lana flicked ashes from her cigarette three times into the sink. "I can't send her to school looking like a tramp. I can't understand why she would do that to herself. Do you?"

"I don't know. It depends. What did she do to her hair?" I could see a stray wisp of hair sticking out under the scarf.

"She butchered it," Lana said.

"Oh, Mom," Cindy groaned. "It's not that bad." She squeezed a cigarette butt until the tobacco squirted out the end. Lana turned away to get her purse and didn't see Cindy lick the tobacco off her finger.

I couldn't see Cindy's hair because she had covered it with a scarf, but I'd heard something—knew something had happened to her. I didn't want to think about it. I wanted to leave, but just as I stood to go, a car horn blared outside. Lana rummaged in her purse and took out a tube of lipstick. Without using a mirror, she drew a line of red across her mouth.

"Did I get it straight?" She bent over the table so Cindy could see her lips.

With her finger, Cindy wiped a smudge from the corner of her mom's lip. "There. That's better. You're good to go."

Lana kissed Cindy's cheek, leaving a red mark. "You know I love you. Now, don't go out or let anyone in the house. You're welcome to stay for supper Clara. I hope you do because I know Cindy could use some company right now. Help yourselves to the hard-boiled eggs in the fridge. Make up some egg salad sandwiches."

Cindy pulled the curtain aside, and we watched her mother get into a BMW. I recognized the guy behind the wheel. "Is that who I think it is?"

Cindy took another butt from the ashtray and rolled it back and forth on the table.

"Is your mother having an affair with Isabel's Dad?" I asked.

"So, what if she is?"

"Does Isabel know?"

"Yeah. Why do you think Isabel is so mean to me? Imagine having that ugly louse for a stepsister. I hope Mom doesn't marry her father. I'd run away if Mom did that. Better to be homeless than with Isabel bitching at me."

"I know what you mean," I said. "Isabel wouldn't be my pick for sister either."

Cindy flicked her mother's cigarette lighter seven times in succession before it ignited, and she could light the cigarette. She tossed the lighter on the table, took a drag before touching the burning end with her finger.

Her fingertip sizzled. The smell of burning tobacco and charred skin made my stomach turn. "Stop. What's wrong with you?" I knocked the cigarette from her hand and put it out, making sure I'd squashed it so she couldn't pick it up and smoke it again. She sucked the end of her finger. I held my stomach. She was grossing me out. "Your finger must hurt? Do you have any ointment for burns or an Aloe Vera plant?"

"I don't need ointment. My finger doesn't hurt that much." She rolled her sleeve, and I saw burn marks on her arms. "Really, I like the pain. It takes me away from myself."

The girl had issues, and I didn't know how to deal with them.

It was beyond me. I wished my math teacher had asked someone else to drop off her homework.

She wiped the black soot from her finger on her jeans and whispered, "Everyone hates me, and I don't know why."

"I don't hate you." It wasn't a lie, but it wasn't the truth. I had no reason to hate her. I just didn't—like her a whole lot.

"Some girls treat me like shit. Like I'm not human, like I don't have any feelings. You've seen them do it. I know you have."

My face flushed. I'd seen the way the other girls treated Cindy, and I'd stood by on occasion and watched them torment her. I felt so ashamed. More than anything, I wanted to escape this smoke-filled house and this sad girl who everyone picked on. What could I say or do? Her sadness overwhelmed me. "Well, there's your homework. Let me know if you need any help. Will you be at school tomorrow?"

"I'm never going back to school. Never," Cindy said before I could escape. "Isabel will kill me if I go back to school."

She buried her head in her arms and cried. I sat back down again. How could I leave her? I racked my brain for something to say, but nothing came to mind. I counted the cigarette butts in the ashtray three times before Cindy stopped crying and wiped her mother's kiss from her cheek.

"Isabel won't kill you," I said. "Isabel is a bully, but she wouldn't dare go that far."

"A few days ago, Isabel and some of the other girls cornered me in the washroom. She yelled at me about her dad and my mom having an affair. Isabel was furious her parents were going to separate. What makes her think I'm the one to blame because her father's an unfaithful turd? They threatened me with a pair of scissors that someone had swiped from the sewing room. I fought them but slipped and hit my head against the sink and cut my lip. One girl, I didn't see who it was, grabbed my hair and yanked it out by the roots."

Cindy's eyes filled with tears as she pulled off the scarf. She ran her hand over a bald spot. It looked raw and sore. With trembling fingers, she combed a tuff of hair, leaving it sticking straight up. The rest was a tangled mess.

"They were going to cut my hair, but they were interrupted by someone flushing the toilet, and they ran out of the washroom," she said in a shaky voice.

My stomach tightened. "Did you…did you see who was in the stall?"

"I might have," Cindy whispered. "I…I wonder why she didn't help me."

I stood to go and placed my sweating hand around the doorknob. God, how I wanted to get out of her house, but I couldn't leave her. I let go of the doorknob. "I think she helped you by flushing the toilet and scaring them away."

"Maybe, but she didn't stop to see if I was okay."

"That was wrong. She should have made sure you were okay. So, why didn't you go to the office and tell the principal what happened?"

"Right. Like that would make things better for me. God, I'm not that stupid."

"Why didn't you tell your mom the truth?"

"Because Mom loves that bitch's father. She needs some happiness in her life, and he's nice to her. My dad never was. So, I told her I cut my hair myself, which I did."

"Why? You could have combed the longer hair over the bald spot because now it—"

"Looks like shit, I know." Cindy shrugged and wrapped the scarf around her head. "I'm ugly anyway. What's the difference?"

I was beginning to understand what was wrong with Cindy. No wonder there were cigarette burns on her arms and scars on her wrists. "One thing about hair, it always grows back," I said. A stupid remark, but I didn't know what else to say. How to deal with her mental state was way beyond me. "If you go back to school, I promise I'll protect you and stick up for you."

"School sucks. I'm never going back."

"But what about your art? You're so talented. I've seen some of your paintings displayed in the hallways. You're always winning awards, and everyone says we have the best art program in the city. So, if you decide to go back to school, I promise to be there for you if you need me. If you get into trouble, I'll help you." She didn't say yes, but she didn't say no, so I took it as a yes. "You know, if you'd trust me to fix your hair, I know I could style it into a cute pixie cut. It would bring out your eyes."

"I don't know…"

I couldn't blame her for not trusting me. After all, I never gave her a moment's notice. "Don't worry. It'll be nice. I promise you. Way better than what you did. My aunt has a hair salon, and she's taught me the basics of a good haircut. I know what I'm doing."

"If you think you could fix it."

"I can. Where do you keep the scissors?"

She pointed to a kitchen drawer, and I rummaged through it until I found a pair of scissors. I hoped they would be sharp enough. I ran the blade over my finger and felt the sharp edge pierce my skin. When I looked up, I saw Cindy watching me as if she knew the scissors were sharp, as if she had used the scissors for more than cutting paper or string. I pulled a chair up to the sink and motioned for her to sit in it. It had a spray nozzle attached to the faucet, which made washing her hair easy. After I combed out her hair, she hopped out of the chair.

"I change my mind," she said. "I think I'll just let it grow out."

"Are you sure? I can make your hair look cool. You won't be sorry." After a moment, she sat back down. She kept her eyes closed until I'd finished cutting her hair. She looked a lot like Tinker Bell in the movie *Peter Pan*. I'd never noticed how pretty she was and how big her eyes were. I looked through my knapsack and found one of my barrettes, a cloisonné bird sitting on a tree branch. I took a tuff of hair and pinned it over the bald spot. When she looked at herself in the mirror, she saw the barrette and smiled. She undid it to examine it and fingered the bird. I'd never seen Cindy smile before.

"It's yours," I said.

"Really?"

It made her so happy you would have thought I had given her a hundred bucks or something. That made me sad. I took the barrette out of her hand and clipped it back into her hair.

Cindy had a passion for birds. She read about them, went bird watching by the river, and included at least one bird in all her paintings. She made birdhouses, too, miniature palaces decorated with acorns, twigs, pretty pebbles, and braided grasses. Six months ago, I saw nine birdhouses hanging from the eaves. Today, I saw only one birdhouse, lying half-hidden by a mound of soggy newspapers.

I picked up the birdhouse and jumped back when a rat darted out of it. Its worm-like tail brushed against my ankle as it scrambled around my feet, frightened by my scream and my step dancing to keep from stepping on it. I didn't know rats could see ghosts. I backed into the door and fumbled for the doorknob. It opened, and I stumbled inside.

The room was dark, and I wondered if I was truly a ghost, then why couldn't I see in the dark. I felt for the light switch and turned it on. All the furniture was gone. Cindy and her mom had moved away and lounging in the breakfast nook and looking rather smug sat Billy.

Chapter Eight

"Hey, babe, you could have walked right through the door." Billy ran his hand through his hair. Static electricity flickered from the roots to the tips.

I'd forgotten I didn't need to open doors anymore, but I didn't like how it felt walking through solid walls. It was like passing through a beaded curtain and having the beads snap back and click against my skin or rather my aura. Energy bouncing off energy is kind of disconcerting. "I like to see where I'm going. Besides, I can't peek around doorways when I'm traveling through them."

"Why don't you just look? The door isn't really there, you know. You should be able to see straight through it, even in the dark.

I turned around and took another look at the door. It had two locks, one a chain and the other a deadbolt. Above the peephole hung a garlic braid to keep the evil spirits out—part of Cindy's Italian heritage. I touched the garlic and the papery shell around the clove crumbled into my hand.

"It's perspective," Billy said. "Like the kaleidoscope. Shift your focus, and you'll see there is no door."

I squinted and rolled my eyes until I became cross-eyed, but I could still see the door.

"Well?"

I shook my head. "The door looks solid to me."

"Interesting. You are earthbound, aren't you?"

He had that right, and I had no intention of leaving the earth and flying off into space or heaven or any other place in between. "Where were you anyway?"

"Surfing a sound wave."

I put my hands on my hips and gave him my best you've got to be kidding, look. "Is that what spirits do for recreation now?"

"Your screams," he explained.

"Funny."

"I was worried about you. You sounded frightened." He motioned for me to sit across from him in the breakfast nook.

I plopped down on the cracked leatherette mended with duct tape in the same spot I sat when I visited Cindy. "So, you knew what happened to me?"

"Of course, I knew."

"Why did you take so long if you knew I was in trouble?"

"Coming to your aid was like trying to capture a sunbeam. One moment I had you, the next, you flickered away. To tell you the truth, I hadn't expected you to get caught in the void or travel into the future."

"How did I end up in the future?"

"Time is a funny thing. While it is linear in the physical world, here it is fluid. I can only guess that on some level, you wanted to know what happened to the people you knew and loved after you died. Imagination is a great vehicle for time travel. "Your imagination is your preview of life's coming attractions."

"You stole that quote from Einstein."

"I did."

"So, I imagined all this."

"Yes and no."

His nebulous answers were starting to irritate me. "Which is it? Yes or no."

"Your experience was real. It will take some time for you to work things out. You see, imagination gives a non-bodied person stability in a physical world. Without imagination, senses are remembered but not actually experienced. The clearer the memory, the more vivid the experience."

Now, I smelled the smoke in Cindy's house. Stale, musty air. Cigarette burn marks appeared like pockmarks etched into the kitchen table. I smelled garlic on my fingertips and felt the cracked leatherette poking through my cargo pants. Memories becoming a reality.

I pulled the curtain aside and looked out the window. The wind used the gate to tap an irregular drumbeat on the backyard fence. Dry leaves spiraled across the yard. I looked up, and the starless sky became filled with stars. Not only my memories but my thoughts could instantly transform my reality. It frightened me to discover how much control I had. Still, if I could imagine stars appearing in the sky, why couldn't I imagine myself back at home in my bed, alive and continuing with my life. "How am I supposed to find the truth if everything is imagined?"

"Truth comes in many forms. The trouble is separating the

chaff from truth's kernel." He traced the burn marks Cindy had etched into the wooden table with her cigarette butts with his index finger. He made them appear and disappear.

"Where did Cindy move to?"

"She didn't come out of a coma."

I took a deep breath and let it out slowly. "What? She didn't die, did she?"

"Her physical body hasn't died yet, but soon. They're talking about taking her off life support. Her mother wants more time. She's moved in with her boyfriend."

"No, really? Isabel's dad? She's not going to like that."

"It's been hard for Lana to accept what has happened."

I stood and paced in front of the stove. The walls buckled, the floor pulsated, and Billy's physical body turned to light. I wiped my eyes, but it wasn't the tears blurring my vision. I needed to work hard to stay focused and keep Billy in view. "When I saw Cindy wandering through Mrs. Kelly's rose garden, was she in a coma?"

"Yes. A lot is happening in a cocoon when it seems nothing is happening at all," Billy said. "She wanted to talk to you. To tell you something."

"I want to see her. Maybe…maybe I can wake her. If she's in the hospital, I can see her if I wish hard enough. Right?"

"You could try."

A thought. That's all it took to propel me to the hospital, where I found myself standing in the doorway to Cindy's room. Marty sat in a chair by her bed. He was reading *Great Expectations* out loud. I listened in the doorway until his voice broke, and he stopped reading and hung his head. His glasses slid down his nose and fell into his lap. I stepped inside the room and listened to the ventilator breathing for Cindy. A scary sound, like Darth Vader. At least they hadn't taken her off life support yet.

"Her hair is a little longer," I said.

He stiffened, picked up his glasses, and put them on. He glanced over his shoulder, blinked, sat back in the chair. He sighed heavily. "What are you doing still hanging around? It's been months."

"I know, but it feels like only a few hours to me. Time is a bit screwy here in la-la-land. Can you see me?"

He placed the book on the side table, stood, and looked out the window. I followed and stood beside him. "Sort of. I can see you as a reflection in the window. You look blurry, transparent, and… far away."

"I'm close, standing beside you, looking out the window with you."

"Damn, you really are a ghost."

"Looks like it, doesn't it?"

He turned toward me. Seeing nothing, he talked to my reflection in the window. "It's not right that you haven't moved on. Go. Get out of here." He slapped his palms against the windowpane as if that might make me disappear. Startled, I jumped back. What happened to the sweet, gentle Marty I used to know?

"Sorry. I don't know why I did that." When he looked me in the eyes, I saw fear, anger, and sadness. A lump rose in my throat. Like Peter and Lucy, Marty needed to forget about me. It hurt too much.

"If you need me to say it, it's okay to go. Look for the tunnel of light and stuff—"

"Stop. That's a bunch of shit. You watch too much TV. It's not like that. It's not like that at all."

"You mean there's no tunnel of light?" He sounded disappointed.

"There's light, but crossing can be more complicated than that. You see, I can't go until I resolve something, and I think it has to do with Cindy. What happened to her?"

"She stepped into a wasps' nest. She had an allergic reaction and went into a coma. I didn't know she was allergic to wasps. Did you?"

"No, I didn't but… but there must be more to it than that. Where was this nest?"

"In the forest by the river."

"That's not on her route home. I thought you were going to walk her home since I couldn't be there because of my audition. You promised me."

"I was a little late, and she didn't wait for me."

"Why? What happened?"

"You still don't know what happened, do you," he said.

"No. Not all of it. How did I die?"

"The bus hit you."

"I know, but I don't understand how or why."

"You ran into the street to help Cindy, I think. She was covered in wasps, and the bus couldn't stop in time."

Why couldn't I remember what happened? "What was she doing down by the river."

"Hell, I don't know. Bird watching?"

Bird watching. That made sense. Still, there was something niggling me.

"Cindy is the only one who knows what happened and …" He cleared his throat. "She's…she's not able to tell us."

"Marty, is there anything else I should know?"

"Like what?"

"Was Peter cheating on me with Isabel?"

He leveled his eyes on mine, and without blinking, said, "I don't know who's telling the truth anymore. Ever since you left, nothing feels right. It's all wrong. You're dead. Cindy is almost dead. Peter is in a bad way. I haven't seen him for months. He quit school, doesn't answer my calls. He's never home when I go by his place." He shook his head. "I don't understand why all of this happened, and talking to you through a pane of glass is making me crazy."

I had so many questions for Marty, but the nurse came in and told him visiting hours were over.

"Okay," he said. He waited for the nurse to go, but she stood in the doorway. "Please, I need a few more minutes." The nurse stepped away, but I could see her shadow darken the hallway floor.

Marty leaned over the bed. "Hey, Cindy, it's time to wake up. Please. Open your eyes." "C'mon. There's not much time left before they take away your life support. C'mon, do it for me." He clutched the blanket and closed his fist around it. "I can't reach her."

His desperation hit me so hard I felt myself flicker.

He stepped back and looked at me. His eyes said he blamed me. "I'm angry. Cindy had such a tough time at school. No one wanted to be her friend. She didn't deserve this."

He ran his hand over the windowpane, and we put our hands together. A pane of glass separated our palms, yet we connected. "Please help her," he whispered in a hoarse voice.

"I can't. I don't know how. Just because I'm dead doesn't mean I can perform miracles."

"Why did you come back here if you can't help her?" He turned away and took Cindy's hand in his, and held it to his heart.

Before I could answer him, the nurse walked into the room and picked up *Great Expectations.* "Don't forget to take your book," she said.

Marty glanced over his shoulder at the nurse. With narrowed eyes and a voice laced with daggers, he said, "Leave it. I'll be back tomorrow." He tucked Cindy's hand under the blanket, leaned over, and kissed her forehead.

"I'm sorry, but her mother has decided to take her off life support. It's time to take your book home." She held out the book. Marty smacked it out of her hand. The book hit the wall and fell open.

The nurse pursed her lips and left the room. I thought Marty would pick it up, but he didn't. Instead, he clenched his fists and turned his back to face the window. His eyes filled with tears. So, did mine.

More than anything, I wanted to reach through the glass and hug him. "I don't know if I can do anything, but I'll try," I said.

"Just be her friend. Okay? Take care of her." Before leaving, he picked up the book and tucked it under his arm.

I backed away from the window and saw Cindy sitting up on the edge of the bed. Not in her body but outside it like me. Both of us ghosts now. I sat beside her.

"Marty cares so much about you," I said.

"Yeah, I love listening to his voice when he reads to me. He makes me want to wake up, but I can't. I wish with all my heart that I could. Mom cries and cries, and I want to tell her I'm okay, but my eyes are stuck shut. Sometimes I can hear people talking and feel words on the tip of my tongue, but I can't speak. It hurts to breathe, and sometimes I feel like I'm suffocating. I'm trapped."

I knew how she felt. I, too, felt trapped in this place between life and death.

"Am I dead?" she asked.

"No. I am. But you're not doing so great." The circles under her eyes were purple. I didn't think she had long to live. "If they take away life support, you have to try to hang on."

"I'm not sure I can. I'm not sure I want to. Mom and Isabel's dad are really tight. She's moved in with him. There's no place for me in Mom's life now."

"C'mon, Cindy. You have so much to live for, your talent for one. What about Marty?"

"I like Marty," For a moment, a thin smile brightened her face.

"I know you do, and I think he likes you."

"Did he say he did?" She looked hopeful.

"He doesn't have to say it. I see how much he cares about you. How often does he come to visit you?"

"Every day."

"There's your answer."

"He feels guilty. He thinks it's his fault because he was late and didn't get to walk me home."

"What happened? Why didn't you wait for him?"

"I don't know. I can't remember. The doctors say I have brain damage. Is that why I can't wake up?"

"Maybe you have amnesia. I hear that happens sometimes. You must remember something."

"I remember it was you," she said.

"Me?" I didn't know what she meant.

"In the washroom when they tried to cut my hair," she said

without emotion, neither accusing or berating me.

Shamed at being caught lying rattled me, and for a moment, I found myself back in Cindy's house sitting in the nook with Billy. I couldn't look at him because he would know. What was I saying? He probably already knew about my lie. I wanted to run and hide. I told myself I didn't have to face her if I didn't want to because soon, she would be dead. I wanted to get away from her but seeing Billy for that one brief second reminded me that I would still have to face myself, and that terrified me even more. A moment later, I found myself back in the hospital room. "You knew all along, but you didn't say anything. Why?"

"Because I knew you were as scared of them as I was and because I wanted you to be my friend." Cindy leaned back on the bed and slipped into her body.

I picked up the cloisonné barrette I had clipped in her hair the day I styled it. Someone had placed it on the table beside a bouquet of white lilies, arranged in a crystal vase etched with sparrows, Cindy's favorite bird. I recognized the vase as the same one I saw sitting empty on the kitchen counter by the fridge in her house. Perhaps the vase was forgotten when Lana moved out.

In an instant, I found myself back in Cindy's kitchen. I grasped the vase and traced the etching of the sparrows with my finger. Billy leaned against the fridge. He didn't smile or frown or ask what happened. It must have surprised him to see me come and go like that, but he didn't say a word about it. With tears streaming down my cheeks, I sobbed out the words one at a time. "I… saw… her."

"She's getting ready to go," he said. "There's nothing you can do."

"But…"

"You can come home too, anytime you're ready."

"I'll never be ready." I opened a cupboard door and saw that it was crawling with black weevils. I slammed it shut. Being angry helped me stop crying. Being angry chased away the shame, eating away at my soul. "I don't want to go with you. I'm not done yet. I haven't done anything with my life. It's been a big waste of time. I was hoping to do something meaningful before I died."

Billy put his hands on my shoulders and turned me to face him. "Life is not about the big splash. It's about the ripple effect of one small pebble."

I pulled away from him. "Shit. You're getting on my nerves." I had to get out of Cindy's house and away from Billy. I opened the door and stepped outside. The night air sweetened by the smell of someone's fireplace calmed me as I stepped out onto the porch. I wished I could go home, sit in front of our hearth with a good book and a cup of hot chocolate topped with whipped cream. The wind had a bite of winter frost on its breath. It nudged me forward and down the porch steps. Billy waited for me on the bottom stair with one foot up on the last step, blocking my way. He'd jumped ahead of me somehow. I guess he didn't want to lose me again.

Gray paint blistered on the porch railing. I peeled off a piece and flicked it into the air. It took flight in the breeze and disappeared. I pushed by Billy, who moved aside as I stomped down the steps. "Go away." I bit my lower lip to keep from crying and walked down the street toward the bus stop. A moment later, I heard Billy following me on his Harley, driving slowly at first, the engine making a throaty rumble. "I mean it. Get lost." I ran ahead and heard the Harley roar. He honked his horn and drove by me.

Chapter Nine

As I drew near the bus stop, I saw a man sitting on the bench, leaning over his knees with his head in his hands. I couldn't make out his features, but the body shape looked familiar. He was wearing a navy jacket, jeans, and high-top sneakers with no laces. I recognized those sneakers and wanted to shout, "Peter, it's me. I'm here," but I didn't want to scare him away like I scared Lucy.

For a few minutes, I stood behind the bench and watched him. He looked miserable: greasy hair, stains on his jeans, and mud caked on his sneakers. In one hand, he held my kaleidoscope, and in the other hand, a cigarette burnt to the filter. The kaleidoscope gave me hope that he would still be able to see and hear me after five months. The cigarette shocked me. I'd never seen Peter smoke. Actually, everything about him confused me. This Peter, I didn't know. He'd changed so much I hardly recognized him as he rolled the kaleidoscope between his hands.

I sat beside him. "Looking for me?"

He looked up and breathed in with a hiss. "Clara?" He raised his hand to touch me, to gather me in his arms, but he stopped outside my aura, dropped his hand, and gripped the edge of the bench. "You're here?"

I wanted to pull him off the bench and make him dance with me even though I knew he didn't like to dance. In my mind, I said, "Please kiss me," out loud I said. "Yes, I'm here." We looked at each other for a moment in silence until it was unbearable, and I blurted out the first thing that came to mind. "What are you doing out here at this hour?"

"Waiting for you."

My heart shattered.

"And you?" He dropped the cigarette butt on the ground and stepped on it.

"Looking for you."

"What took you so long?" He sounded angry, hurt. "I come here every day hoping to see you again. Why didn't you come back?" He ran his hand over the stubble on his cheeks—a half beard, which made him look a little seedy.

"Time is strange for me in this realm. What seems like five months to you feels like a few hours to me. I'm sorry. I would have come sooner if I could. I didn't know how. Yesterday, today, tomorrow, it's all the same to me now," I said, borrowing Billy's words.

"I wish we could turn back time," he said.

"Me too. Can you still see me?"

He looked at me for a long time, and I looked at him, memorizing every line, dimple, and freckle on his face. Peter didn't have to say he could see me. I knew he could because he looked me in the eyes, and Peter didn't do that the first time he saw me after I'd died. "I guess the kaleidoscope still works."

"Do you want it back?" He held it out.

I pushed it toward him. "No, keep it. Keep it so you can see me because I'm never going to leave you. Never."

"I don't want you to do that. You need to be free of me."

My stomach sank. Peter didn't want me to hang around and see him live out his life. To love someone else.

"Marty's right. You need to move on," he added. The words were like a knife to my heart.

"I don't want to move on. I want to stay a part of your life. Why did you quit school?"

"How do you know that? Have you been watching me?"

"No. Marty told me. I saw him at the hospital. He's worried about you."

"School wasn't working for me anymore. The memories were everywhere. Your locker, our favorite table in the cafeteria, and the flute section in the band. I walked the halls like a zombie wishing I'd stayed at the bus stop with you instead of riding away on Marty's bike."

He rested his arm on the bench behind me, almost a hug. I wanted him to hug me, to wrap his arm, solid and warm, around my shoulders. "Talk to me. Tell me what's been happening. You don't look yourself."

"I miss you," he said.

"Not as much as I miss you." I inched my hand toward his knee and touched the seam of his jeans. He looked at my hand. I moved it away and clasped my hands together so he wouldn't see them shaking.

"I got into a bit of trouble and had to move out of my dad's place. I have a room downtown."

"What kind of trouble?"

"It's a long story, and… well…you don't need to know about it now."

"Yes, I do. How can you say that? Did you think I would stop caring about you just because—"?

"You died?"

What could I say? Yeah, I'm dead, but why would that change anything? Apparently, it did—to him. I wanted to say I love you so much, and death will never change that. I swallowed the words and said, "Tell me. Please, I need to know what happened."

He bounced his knee until I put my hand on it. This time I didn't let it go straight through. I had more control now. He placed his hand over mine.

"Marty and I went to the party at Isabel's house, the one you didn't go to." He mumbled, speaking so quietly I strained to hear him.

"The one I wasn't invited to."

"Well, Marty wanted to go because Ashley was there, and he convinced me to go with him. Isabel was drinking a lot. You know her mom was out of town and all. So, anyway, we ran out of food and drinks, and she was going to take her mom's car to the store to get some more snacks. She was smashed, and I didn't want her to drive. We argued until she agreed to let me go with her, but she insisted on driving. On the way home from the store, she ran into a homeless person. Shit, he bounced off the car, and his shopping cart looked like a tangled mess of barbed wire. Have you ever heard a body hit a moving car?"

"No, but my dad hit a deer once. It was awful. One hoof came right through the windshield."

"God," he moaned. "It would have sounded a lot like that. It's a miracle the crash didn't kill you."

"Yeah, a miracle. Too bad there weren't a few more of those to go around." Like a cat, I had used up all my nine lives. "Did the homeless guy die?" I remembered something about the accident in the news, but I didn't pay any attention to it.

"His name's Hal, and no, he didn't die, but his injuries were life-threatening. It's been over six months, and he's still in the hospital. What a nightmare it's been. The crash, you dying, and my dad going ballistic."

"Tell me about it. I'm still in the middle of my nightmare."

He squeezed my hand, still resting on his knee. "Anyway, Isabel couldn't stop crying, so she let me drive. She made up this elaborate story about how the car was stolen and made me park it on another street. We walked home, and I called 911 on my cell and reported the accident. I knew it wasn't right to leave him on the street to die."

"Did they connect Isabel's mom's car to the accident?"

"Yeah, an accident that bad leaves behind evidence. Isabel told the police that someone stole the car when her mom was out of town."

"The police traced me by my cell number, and when they questioned Isabel, she told them I stole the car and that she was protecting me. She convinced Tina and Ashley to say I stole the car because we fought at the party. We did fight, but I didn't steal the car."

I let go of Peter's hand and stood. I couldn't sit anymore, not when I wanted to deck Isabel. I paced the length of the bench and back. "I'm going to haunt her. I'll find her and scare the shit out of her until she confesses."

Peter stood and took my hands in his. "No. I don't want you to do that," he said and pulled me into a hug.

The hug surprised me. I couldn't speak at first. "Why are you protecting Isabel?" My words were muffled by his coat, which smelled as musty as a wet dog. I didn't care. I would have stayed with my head resting on his musty chest forever if I could.

"I'm not. I was protecting you." He held me tighter.

"Me?"

"Yes. Always. That was the reason I didn't tell you in the first place. I knew it would upset you."

It hadn't occurred to me that Peter's silence was his way of shielding me or sparing my feelings.

"Don't be haunting people on my account. Isabel's not worth black marks on your soul." He kissed the top of my head.

Black marks on my soul for a haunting? Is that what happens? I'd have to ask Billy the next time I saw him, that is if he was still speaking to me.

We swayed, wrapped in each other's arms, underneath the lamplight. A slow two-step shuffle, almost a dance. Peter hummed a melody I'd never heard before.

I lifted my head and asked, "What's that song? " His eyes were closed, his face looked more relaxed than I'd seen it in a long while.

"I wrote it for you. No lyrics yet. I can't seem to come up with the right words."

"You will. You can't rush these things. And Peter, I don't want you to protect me. I want you to share everything with me, the good and the bad. Did anyone see you leave the party?"

"Only Marty, everyone else was either playing video games or making out somewhere." He released me, and we sat on the bench, still holding hands. His were clammy. Did he find my hands cold? "Marty told the police he saw us leave together, but it's his word against everyone else's. I was arrested and spent the night in a cell. My old man got me out of jail. When we got home, he freaked at me, saying stuff like I ruined his reputation at work and how could I do this to him? He wouldn't listen to my side of the story, so I left. It's for the better. He was making me crazy with his unpredictable moods."

"Where are you staying?"

"Eastside. I play my guitar and sing on the streets sometimes for money. It's not over, though. I have to go to court."

"When?"

"Tomorrow. But I'm not going. That's why I wanted to see you tonight. Because I'm leaving, and I may never come back here again."

"You can't run away. You must stick up for yourself. You need to tell the police Isabel was driving."

"No one will believe me."

"You have to go to court and tell them what happened. Tell them your side of the story. Plead not guilty."

"I can't win this. It's Isabel's word against mine, and her mother is a lawyer."

"You can do this. You have to try."

"What's the point? When you left, you took my heart with you, and without it, I'm nothing."

"Don't say that," I whispered. "Don't let what happened to

me stop you from living. That will make me feel terrible. If you love me, you will try to be the musician you always dreamed you'd be. You'll finish the words to my song."

I heard the bus before I saw it come around the corner. I resented its squeaky breaks interrupting our time together. It stopped in front of us, and a girl I had never seen before stepped out and sat on the bench beside Peter. She looked pretty enough, but she chewed her gum as if her life depended on it, and she had too much black liner around her eyes. I hated the way she snuggled close to Peter.

I let go of his hand. "I wanted to share my life with you like we dreamed of—forever. Now, it looks like you took your heart back and gave it to someone else."

"Never, my heart is yours forever," he said.

"And mine is yours," the girl said. She poked at a hole in the knee of his jeans, touching his skin with her finger. Her voice, deeper and huskier than I expected, had the tone of someone who smokes too much and lives too hard. Desperate, like Peter. She needed Peter in a different way than I needed him, and that kind of need was not real love. At least that was what I had to tell myself because if I didn't, I might as well find my way back to the void and stay there. Loving Peter and seeing him with another girl broke me in ways I knew would never heal, not here on earth or in the afterlife. Now, I could see why the living had to let go of the dead, and the dead had to let the living live.

"What did you find out?" Peter wrapped his arm around her. I couldn't stand it. I wanted to pull her away from him.

"Ben said he would give us a ride. He has work driving a moving van out of town. Three days drive, he said. We could ride with him, and he'll pay us if we help unload."

"Great. When do we leave?"

"Early tomorrow morning. Ben wants to be on the road by dawn."

"Peter, don't run," I said. His arm held her, but his eyes held me. I wanted to say, hug me with your eyes, Peter and never let me go.

"What's wrong?" she asked.

He turned away from me. "Nothing. I was just thinking of something."

"You mean someone. Clara." She spit a wad of gum onto the sidewalk.

"Yeah."

"Do you still come to her shrine to talk to her?" She pulled away from him and folded herself in her jean jacket. She would never completely have his heart, and she knew it.

"Sometimes." He looked right at me. "And I will always love her."

"Let's go, Peter. It's cold out here." She took his hand and pulled him off the bench. He tucked the kaleidoscope in his pocket. Maybe one day, he would try to use it to reach me again.

I was dead to Peter, and Peter was dead to me. If Billy hadn't arrived on his Harley, I would have followed Peter and his new girlfriend and shamelessly haunted her for a few more hours. I didn't care if haunting her would put black spots on my soul.

Billy turned off the engine and met me in front of the shrine. I saw my picture still propped against the lamppost and one unlit candle cradled by a ring of winter pansies. I smiled at the yellow mums from Mom and Dad. Nothing said Peter to me. Freddie was gone. I hoped Marty still had him. "Soon, they will all forget me."

"They will never forget, but you don't want them to grieve for you forever, do you?" Billy said.

Yeah, I did, but I couldn't admit it to Billy. I knew he was right, but I still wasn't ready to let go.

"They're moving forward, Clara. So must you."

"What now?"

"It's up to you."

"What are my choices?"

He opened his arms wide. "Anything you can imagine."

"If I can travel ahead in time, can I travel backward?"

"Why would you want to do that?"

"To change something."

"Your death?"

"Can I?"

"The thread of your present life ended at the bus stop."

He made it sound so final. Dismayed, I plopped on the bench. He sat beside me. "So, I can't change anything."

"I didn't say that."

"What are you saying? Can I, or can't I?"

"It's possible but complicated. You see, if you go back and relive your past, you won't remember you died in the future. You won't remember me."

"But right now, I'm five months in the future, and I remember the past," I said.

"You can remember the past because it already happened, but you will not remember the future because it hasn't happened yet."

"What? I don't get it. Why doesn't it work both ways?"

"That's the rules," he said. "Some things I can change, some I can't. Do you know for sure what's going to happen to you in the next few hours or days?"

Now, I could see the problem. Unless I were psychic, I wouldn't know what would happen. "But in the movie *Back to the Future*—"

"This isn't a movie, Clara. It's real life."

"Real life?"

"You know what I mean. When you go back into the past, you'll have a clean slate to work with."

I sighed. "Are you sure? I've read many time travel stories where people go back in time and remember what they need to do to make a difference. And…and Einstein said that past, present, and future is just a persistent illusion."

"What do you think he meant by that?" Billy asked.

"Well…" I began. I wasn't exactly sure what Einstein meant, but I wanted to believe that time was simultaneous. I hoped that Einstein had discovered the one thing that meant I could still be alive. I wanted to believe that on some level, somewhere, somehow, I was still alive and carrying on with my life. If I could find that place, that person I once was or could be in the future or the past, I didn't care which one, I could slip back into myself. "Reality is timeless," I said, still unsure of myself. "What do you think it means?"

Billy rustled the change in his pocket, and finally, after a few awkward moments, he turned to me with eyes so compassionate I thought I would burst out crying. "It is hard when you are in the third dimension to see time as anything other than linear." He cleared his throat a few times before continuing." If you stand outside of time, you see it as a conglomeration of events all happening at once, so in a sense, you are correct when you say all time is simultaneous. In truth, time is all a matter of perspective, like the kaleidoscope. When you turn a wheel, there is a birth. When you turn it again, there is a death, and there is just a single sliver of glass difference between them."

Billy's explanation made me shiver. I pulled my fingers into the sleeves of my sweater so he couldn't see my hands shaking. Where was this place where time could appear like a tangled-up ball of yarn? I bit my lip to keep from crying but could not stop the tears pooling in my eyes.

"Billy, if you know everything about me, why don't you just tell me why I'm stuck here?"

"You're not stuck. I've shown you the way a couple of times. You refuse to go. Do you know why?"

"No. Just tell me, and we can go."

"If I told you, would knowing make a difference? Would you follow the yellow brick road and off to Oz we'll go?"

"Damn, you make me want to scream. You could at least give me one small hint so that I can change things for Cindy and Peter."

"Just for Cindy and Peter?"

Billy had a way of asking me the hard questions. Did I want to do this just for Cindy and Peter? No. I wanted to live, and if I could change something for Cindy, then maybe I could change the outcome for myself, for Lucy, Mom, Dad, and Peter. "For all of us," I whispered. "Can I do that? For everyone?"

"Maybe, but there are many roads in a person's journey. Some are irreversible. These are the agreed-upon markers, like your birth and death. Both will happen at a certain point. Notice I didn't say time. Death is an exit point, not a time, and it can happen for many different reasons, some accidental. Do you understand?"

"Not really."

"If a person has three things to accomplish, and they accomplish them in life, then death's exit kicks in. Most people have a grocery list of things to do, though."

"Did I?"

"Your list was very short."

I didn't like Billy's philosophy. "So, I was supposed to die."

"I didn't say that. Some people have short lists but live a long time because it takes many experiences to fulfill their desires. Cindy had a long list that she didn't get a chance to complete."

"Will you help me? I want to try to make a change that would allow Cindy to live and complete her list."

"It won't be easy, and normally this isn't done. You see, there are so many things that can change the final outcome, and it doesn't have to be something big. A slight change in the course of events can make a huge difference. You will be at the mercy of everyone around you. I'm willing to let you try if it brings you home."

Home. Where was my home now? Not on Carlyle Boulevard, where my mom and dad, and little sister lived.

"If you relive your last few hours, I'd say less than ten, then we can narrow down the probability that someone else will interfere with what you are trying to do. The smallest, most insignificant choice by anyone could affect the outcome for better or worse."

"What could be worse? I'm dead. I've lost everything, and everyone, including Peter and Cindy, is close to death. How do I make a change if I can't remember what I did?"

"By remembering what's important."

"Billy, if I can't remember what's important or what I did in the first place, it will all play out the same. Won't it? I'll still be the same person, thinking the same things and making the same choices as before. Unless something changes, it will be a big waste of time. Everything will turn out the same, and I'll end up dead, standing at the bus stop with a badass biker for a guide."

His eyes had always had an eerie light, to begin with, but now they looked straight through me. "Is that who you think I am? Just because I like to ride a Harley, wear leather, and have a tattoo on my arm doesn't mean I'm a bad person. You jump to conclusions without knowing who I am. Not all bikers are hellraisers."

I stood and walked across the street to Al's Grocery and tried the door even though I knew it was closed. Hell, I could walk right through that door if I wanted. And I did. I walked up and down the aisles, looking at nothing. I thought about Cindy and how we judged her by her clothes and hair without knowing her. We never saw her incredible talent at art. I turned down the soft drink aisle and saw Billy at the end, blocking my way. He opened a glass coke bottle with his teeth and spat out the metal cap. He took a long gulp and wiped his mouth with the back of his hand.

The metal cap clinked and rolled toward me. I kicked it back toward him and he stepped on it. It disappeared under his foot. "So, did you really think I was escorting you to hell?"

"Yes, it crossed my mind. Are you?" I took a deep breath. I'm not sure I wanted the answer.

He laughed. "Hey babe, how bad have you been?" He snatched a bag of cheese twists off the shelf, and threw it at me.

I caught the bag in midair. "I thought you knew everything about me."

"I do, but I'm curious to know what you think you did that's worthy of hell."

There were so many things eating me up right now that I couldn't choose only one. I placed the unopened bag on the shelf with the ripple potato chips and buried my head in my hands.

"That bad?" he asked.

When I didn't answer him, he rested his hand on my shoulder. "Okay, I'll help you," he said softly.

I swallowed the lump lodged in my throat and whispered, "Thanks."

"Hey, what are Light-Keepers for?"

"So, how are we going to do this?" I asked.

"Hmmm, let me think about this for a moment." He closed his eyes, and when he opened them again, he said, "We'll have to improvise as we go along. Like a jazz riff." He walked through the wall and out onto the sidewalk. After taking a deep breath, I followed.

The bus pulled up and stopped in front of the store. The doors swished open. Billy motioned for me to follow him. "Let's take the bus."

"Not this bus Billy. I know where this bus goes, and it doesn't go back in time. Anyway, I've never heard of traveling back in time on the bus."

"There are other ways to time travel. For me to travel to the past, it would take a mere thought, but for you who is on death's shore, the options are limited. I don't suppose you'd like to take my Harley."

As tempting as it sounded, getting on Billy's motorbike frightened me. I shook my head no.

"I didn't think so. We'll take the bus then." He urged me forward with a smile and a wave of his hand.

Chapter Ten

How crazy was this? Taking a bus to the past? An ordinary everyday bus, except the bus, was empty, and no one was driving it. Okay, not so ordinary. Was this a real bus or a ghostly bus? I could smell the diesel exhaust and feel the engine rumbling beneath me. My finger brushed a piece of gum stuck to the side of a pole. Real. Definitely real. So, where was the bus driver? "Are you driving?" I asked Billy.

"No, you are," he said.

"What? No way. You'll have to drive it. I don't have the faintest idea how."

"This is your journey, Clara. I'm just along for the ride."

The dude must be nuts to think I could drive a bus. Even if I could, I wouldn't. It's against the law. I know, I know, I'm dead, but it's still against the law. "Forget it. I'm not driving it. You need a special license to drive a bus, and I don't even have a car license. Not even my learners."

"Do you want to do this or not?"

"I do, but I'm not a good driver. My Dad let me back the car out of the driveway once, but I drove right over the lawn and into my mom's flower garden. He said I should wait until I'm eighteen, and I agree with him. Driving a car or bus is one thing, but time travel is way beyond me. I love math and physics, and I'm sure a brilliant scientist will calculate the formula for time travel one day, but as far as I know, no one has worked that out yet. Besides, if I drive, we could end up in Shakespeare's time or during the black plague or worse, before man walked the earth."

Billy laughed. "Backing up isn't easy for most drivers, including the experienced ones. Don't worry. We're going to drive forward, not backward."

"Forward into the past? That makes perfect sense."

"I promise you, no backing up or parallel parking."

Silly of me to get all panicky, but earth's rules were hard to shake. I told him again, "I don't have a license."

"On earth, you need a license. On the road to the past, all you need is a responsible adult to drive with you. Like me."

"You?"

"Yes, like when you get your learners. No driving after midnight and always with an adult with a valid driver's license."

"I don't think your license is still valid. Besides, it's for a motorcycle, not a bus."

"Do you really think the cosmic police are going to arrest you and put you in jail?"

I told myself to quit being silly, drive the stupid bus and get on with it. But I couldn't. Why? The fear of failure? The fear of death? I mean, the fear of death forever and ever amen.

"Ready?" he asked.

"As ready as I'll ever be." Driving the bus felt like one of those things I didn't want to do but had to, like going to the dentist to get a tooth filled. I sat in the driver's seat and looked for the emergency brake just in case we needed to stop in a hurry. The bus was idling, a rough chugging sound. I gripped the wheel. What did my dad tell me? Hands at ten o'clock and two o'clock. No, the new way was nine o'clock and three o'clock. My knuckles turned white as I pressed the gas pedal. The air brakes hissed as they released, and the bus squeaked as it moved forward. I hated the nauseating rotten egg smell of diesel.

"Easy," Billy held onto the pole behind me.

"Whoa…we're moving." Compared to my dad's car, it drove like a tank. It was both thrilling and scary. There were other cars on the road, but I didn't know if the drivers could see us or not. No one passed us or honked their horn, which was a miracle because I was driving slowly, slower than most buses. "Which way?"

"Take any route you like. All roads end up, well…in the same place."

I kept to the straight roads and the right-hand turns. No point stressing over left-hand turns if I didn't have to. Going around the block would be the easiest route for me.

Just when I thought I was getting the hang of it, someone sounded their horn. Billy yelled, "Stop," like my father did when I drove over the lawn. Startled, I took my hands off the wheel. The bus swerved into oncoming traffic, and we narrowly missed hitting an SUV. I saw kids riding in the back seat. Billy leaned over me and steered the bus onto the shoulder. The wheels crunched gravel as we slowed to a stop.

I couldn't stop shaking. "Don't yell at me like that. I can't think when people yell at me. I could have crashed into that SUV. You scared me." God, my nerves were frayed.

"Yes, you could have. Didn't you see the stop sign?" My Light-Keeper looked and sounded frazzled.

"No, What stop sign?" I looked behind me.

"You drove right through it."

"Oh…sorry. Good thing there were no cops around."

"Good thing you didn't hit anyone."

"Seriously? Can I?" I looked at Billy. "What's the big deal? Aren't we dead?"

"You are, but they aren't. Watch where you're going."

Nothing made sense in this in-between place where I felt like part ghost and part breathing dreaming sixteen-year-old girl whose worst day up until now was waking up with a zit on her nose. "Isn't this a ghostly bus? What are we doing traveling on a real bus, a real bus with me driving?"

"Like you, the bus is not physical. Since we're traveling just inside death's door, we can have a physical impact on people. Some folks will see the shadow of our bus and mistake it for something else, a car or an animal crossing the road. If they're startled, they could crash."

"You mean I could have killed someone? Oh my God, there were kids in the SUV. You want their deaths on my conscience as well as everything else?" My dad was right. Driving was like holding a loaded gun in your hand. I stood and pushed past Billy and sat on a seat in the middle of the bus. I'd had enough. I wasn't driving.

Billy crouched in the aisle beside me.

I looked out the window so I wouldn't have to look into his

strange eyes—those damn eyes that pulled me away from myself. "Don't make me drive the bus."

"It's your choice, but this is the easy part. If you can't do this, there's no point in trying to go back and change the past."

"Is there another way to go? If we take your Harley, will you drive?"

He gave me a hard-edged look and stood. "No, and I never let anyone drive my hog." Then he smiled and said, "but I'll make an exception for you."

What made the crazy dude think that I could drive a motorcycle which was way more dangerous than driving a bus? Did he think this was a game? I hoped not because this journey to the past was a matter of life and death in more ways than one.

"It sure would be a lot more fun than driving this gutless old tank," he said. "Besides, there's nothing like riding a hog to make you feel more alive, and it's not just the smell of gasoline, the engine's roar, or the wind blowing in your face. It's living life on the edge, and when you're living on the edge, you're in the moment, and when you're in the moment, well, it's pure joy."

"Joy, when you're dead?"

"More so."

I couldn't tell if the dude was fanatical or just plain nuts. Probably both, which didn't bode well for me. I bit my lip and weighed my options. The bus, the Harley, the path of light to God knows where. I stood, walked to the front of the bus, and sat in the driver's seat. I gripped the wheel at nine and two, pressed the gas pedal, and steered the bus back onto the street. I couldn't see how taking this bus around the block would get us back to the past, but I had to trust it would.

"Let's take the bus out of town." Billy made a gesture for me to go left at the next corner. "We'll find a back road where you can get the speed up to make the shift into the realm where we can move through time."

I signaled left and watched the string of traffic going by. I panicked. I kept thinking —now? Should I go now? I was like a deer mesmerized by the headlights. Billy mumbled something about waiting until the road was clear just before I made the leap. Or rather the skid. I floored the gas pedal. The tires squealed as I sped out onto the street and squeezed the bus between two oil tankers.

Billy called on the almighty, but I couldn't tell if he was swearing or praying. "I told you to wait. What were you thinking?"

I smiled to myself. Billy sounded like Dad when Mom was driving. She hated his backseat driving, and the only time I heard them yell at one another was when Dad was having backseat driving road rage. "No worries. There was loads of space between the tankers. If you don't like my driving, you should take the wheel."

I turned onto a dirt road, one that looked like it went on forever in a straight line. It would have been easier to steer the bus on a paved street, but I knew this dirt road, and it was used mainly by the local farmers during the day and the city kids at night when they were out cruising. I pressed the gas pedal, and the bus lurched forward.

"Easy, a little at a time," Billy said, hanging onto the pole. I wondered if his knuckles had turned as white as mine.

Gravel crunched under the bus's wheels, and pebbles rose to pound on the sides. The awful racket wore on my nerves, now so brittle I could almost hear them snapping.

So far, so good. I hadn't hit anyone or anything. I relaxed and pressed the gas pedal a little harder. I had to admit I liked the speed and wished the windows were open so the wind would blow my hair in my face like I imagined it would feel on a Harley. But with my luck, I'd get hammered in the eye with a rock. A second after I thought about getting hit by a rock, one hit the windshield and made me jump. A spider's web spread across the glass. I'd have to be careful about my thoughts becoming a reality. "How fast should we go?"

"The speed of light."

I took a deep breath. "What do you think this bus is? The starship Enterprise?"

"For our purposes, it is. Clara's starship. Get ready to engage the pedal to the metal."

I floored it. The speedometer was as high as it could go, yet the bus continued to speed up.

We went over a bump and then another and another, not rocks but air currents like when you're coming in for a landing and the airplane hits turbulence. I raised my hands in the air, and the steering wheel moved back and forth on its own.

I gripped it anyway, at nine and two. Or should it be nine and three? Whatever, I held on. There was a burst of light, and I shouted, "What's happening? Oh God, I think we're breaking apart." I didn't like feeling discombobulated. Dead or not, it freaked me out big time.

"Hang on," Billy said. "The shift in time is uncomfortable, but it won't last long, just until we cross the threshold."

Uncomfortable was an understatement. One moment I felt physically drained, like when I've danced a long routine, and my body is so tired all my muscles scream to stop. It's all I can do to force myself to keep dancing and do one last grand jeté. I push through the pain to make the leap into the air and extend my legs. Something happens, a shift that makes every step after that weightless and graceful. Going across the threshold felt like that, sort of like Lucy being in the zone.

A calmness settled over us as the bus floated inside what appeared to be a multifaceted jewel, a geometric design I had never seen before. I was in awe. I had so many questions. I took my hands off the wheel and turned in my seat. "What happened?" I asked Billy. "Where are we? What is this geometric pattern? It's so beautiful."

Billy smiled, "What you are seeing hasn't been discovered yet, but when it is, it will become the foundation for space and time travel. Suffice it to say we have stepped outside of space and time.

Billy motioned for me to put my hands back on the wheel. "Except earth's rules don't apply in this dimension. Imagination and will does. Do you remember what Einstein said about imagination?"

"'Imagination is everything,'" I said. "'It is the preview to life's coming attraction.'"

We traveled faster than the speed of light, yet it felt as if we were not moving at all. I looked through the windshield at the jewel-shaped bubble surrounding us. Scenes of places and people from my life flashed across the surface of the jeweled facets outside the bus.

Lucy is running a race at school. She is leading, but just before crossing the finish line, another student comes from behind and wins. Lucy comes in second. She wipes tears from her eyes, and when her friend Janie tries to comfort her, Lucy tells her to get lost. It's sad to see her act like a poor sport.

Marty visits Cindy at the hospital. "Wake up, Cindy," he says. "Open your eyes. Please, do it for me."

My mother is sitting at the dining room table with a single candle burning in front of her. My dad comes home and stands in the doorway. The candlelight flickers shadows across his tired face.

"I made a special meal for us," Mom says and pushes her dinner plate away untouched. "You said you'd be home on time for supper."

Dad doesn't say a word.

"Jake, I can't do this anymore," Mom says. "You're never home. You and me, we might be finished."

"No," I shout at the windshield. "Don't fight because of me."

Next, I see Peter busking outside our favorite café playing his guitar and singing. The gum-chewing girl with the black eyeliner puts a dollar in his guitar case. He looks up and smiles at her.

The scene changes, and Peter's dad, dressed in his business suit, clenches his fist and takes a swing at Peter. Peter grabs his forearm and pushes him into the kitchen table. His dad yells, "Get out. You're not my son."

Our band class is playing Beethoven's, "Ode to Joy," at the annual music festival. The band sounds out of tune.

Ashley blows out the candles on her birthday cake. Her friends, including Tina and Isabel, are singing "Happy Birthday." It must be May 31st. We're getting closer.

My dad is standing over a grave covered in a mound of flowers. There's no gravestone, but I know the grave is mine. He is alone.

It is late afternoon, and Isabel, Ashley, and Tina run in and out of the light streaming through the trees. They climb down the embankment near our school.

"She's there," Tina points toward the river.

"Where?" Ashley asks.

"I saw her running through the trees," Tina says.

"C'mon. This way," Isabel pushes branches out of her way and leads them down to the shore.

Cindy is weaving in and out of the brushwood by the river. She is crying and breathing heavily.

Before I can stop it, I'm drawn toward her, and I'm looking through her eyes even though I'm still seated on the bus with Billy. How weird to be thrust out of a light-body and into a hot, sweaty one. It takes me a moment to get my bearings and become accustomed again to flesh and bones. The hardest part is surfacing from the muddy waters of Cindy's emotions. My mind is overwhelmed. My body, I mean Cindy's body, is sluggish.

Looking through Cindy's eyes is like watching a movie shot with a handheld camera. One moment the ground is a blur of forest lichens, moss-covered logs, and lumpy tree roots meandering across the path. The next moment I see patches of sky through the sun-drenched trees.

Billy squeezes my shoulder. "Pull away, Clara."

Impossible. Cindy's thoughts and feelings become mine. While I have a sense of myself, I also experience every thought, emotion, and physical sensation that Cindy feels. Her panic, her burning leg muscles, her sprained ankle. I can't help but cry out in pain, raw and as real as if it's my own. To be me and someone else at the same time is discombobulating. I hear Billy's voice in the background, nagging me to stop. I can't. I want to tell him what is happening to me, but I think he knows.

Cindy runs along the riverbank, trips, and catches herself. She looks over her shoulder at the afternoon light zigzagging through the green-leafed sky. Ashley, Isabel, and Tina crash through the brushwood stripping the saplings of their branches and leaves to keep from falling. Their muffled voices drift on the breeze.

Cindy's heartbeat drums in my ears. Wild-eyed with panic, she turns a full circle, searching for a safe place to hide. The girls see her. They surround her on all but the river's edge, the worse section where the spring run-off is too high and the current too fast to cross.

"Is this about the bra?" Cindy's thoughts flashback to an incident that happened at the store where Cindy worked. Silly really. It was all about the bra Cindy caught Ashley shoplifting. Ashley tried to hide the sexy little piece of lace under her bra, but Cindy had counted the number of bras Ashley had taken into the dressing room and found that the black one was missing. Cindy told her boss, who confronted Ashley when she tried to leave the store. Embarrassed and humiliated, Ashley pleaded with Cindy's boss not to call the police. She didn't, but Ashley had to pay for the bra.

"Your boss sent my picture to other dress shops like I'm a criminal or something. My mom saw it. Because of you, I'm in big trouble." Ashley has a thin branch in her hand, and she whips Cindy across the ankles. Cindy steps back. Ashley beats her again and again.

Billy continues to nag me like an irritating fly in my face. He wants me to pull away from Cindy. I won't. I can't leave Cindy to fight the bullies on her own.

Cindy clenches her fists and turns to take them on. Isabel lunges at her and grabs the front of her shirt, my blouse, the yellow and green one I wore that day. I can't recall why Cindy is wearing it. It's made of cotton and rips easily.

"You bitch," I say, or rather Cindy and I say together. She grabs Isabel's arm and digs in her nails. Warm blood gushes under her fingertips. It must hurt because Isabel roars a series of curses, I'd never dream of stringing together. With a yank, she lets go of Cindy's hair. Before Cindy can escape, Tina shoves Cindy in the chest. Cindy stumbles backward, staggers, and grabs a willow branch to keep from falling. Tina pushes Cindy again, knocking her onto her back against a sharp-edged rock. She winces and stifles a cry.

"Get up, get up," I say.

She rolls onto her knees and stands, hunched over and panting. She clenches her fists and braces herself to fight even though she can't win. I urge her to "run, run, run."

Cindy swings her foot and kicks Ashley in the knee, the perfect place to wound a dancer. I'm cheering. Ashley screams and screws up her face like a wrinkled old bulldog.

"Go Cindy Go," I'm becoming more frantic with each moment. I hope they don't kill her. Enough is enough. They made their point, so why aren't they backing off?

They follow Cindy up the incline with Isabel in the lead. She grabs the back of Cindy's shirt and spins her around. Cindy balls her fist and hits Isabel in the stomach. Tina grabs Cindy's arm and twists it behind her back. She pushes her down the incline, headlong into a wild blackberry bush near the water's edge.

Cindy thrashes her way through the brambles. Thorns pierce her skin, oh no, not just thorns— wasps. Hundreds of wasps cover her face, arms, and hands. She tries to scrape them off, but they're everywhere, buzzing and biting. Her eyelids, lips, and tongue swell. The balls of her feet and armpits swell too. With her lungs aching for air, she crawls up the embankment. I can't breathe and have to pull away from Cindy's mind. My cries become muffled in Billy's arms.

Breaking the link with Cindy's mind is like waking from a night terror. I had them all the time when I was little and would wake up with my dad's arms around me, like Billy's arms wrapped around me now.

"It's okay, you're safe," He sounded like my dad. Silly, I didn't need to breathe air anymore, yet I'd felt like I was suffocating.

I pulled away from him, embarrassed to be clinging to him like a child. "It was horrible," I said over and over again. What I'd seen and experienced with Cindy sickened me. I had no idea what Cindy had gone through that day. Billy took my arm, pulled me from the driver's chair, and placed me in a passenger seat. "My turn to drive," he said and sat down to take the wheel.

I dried my tears with the edge of my sleeve. "Where are we going?"

"Back a few hours," Billy said.

We traveled on the dirt road again with rocks rumbling against the sides of the bus. Billy drove the bus around the block once before stopping in front of my house. I looked out the window. First-light glowed on the horizon. A new day. My new day. A light turned on in my neighbor's house. A moment later, they let the dog out.

When I stood to go, Billy placed his hands on my shoulders and turned me to face him. "Are you sure?" he asked.

"Dead sure." My voice trembled at my stupid joke. Billy didn't smile. "How will I get back to you?"

"There's only one way."

The fear of death stabbed through me as surely as if I were still alive. I hadn't considered the possibility of reliving my death, and secretly I hoped I wouldn't have to. If I could change things for Cindy, maybe I could change things for myself. With all my heart, I hoped Billy was wrong as I stepped off the bus and into the past.

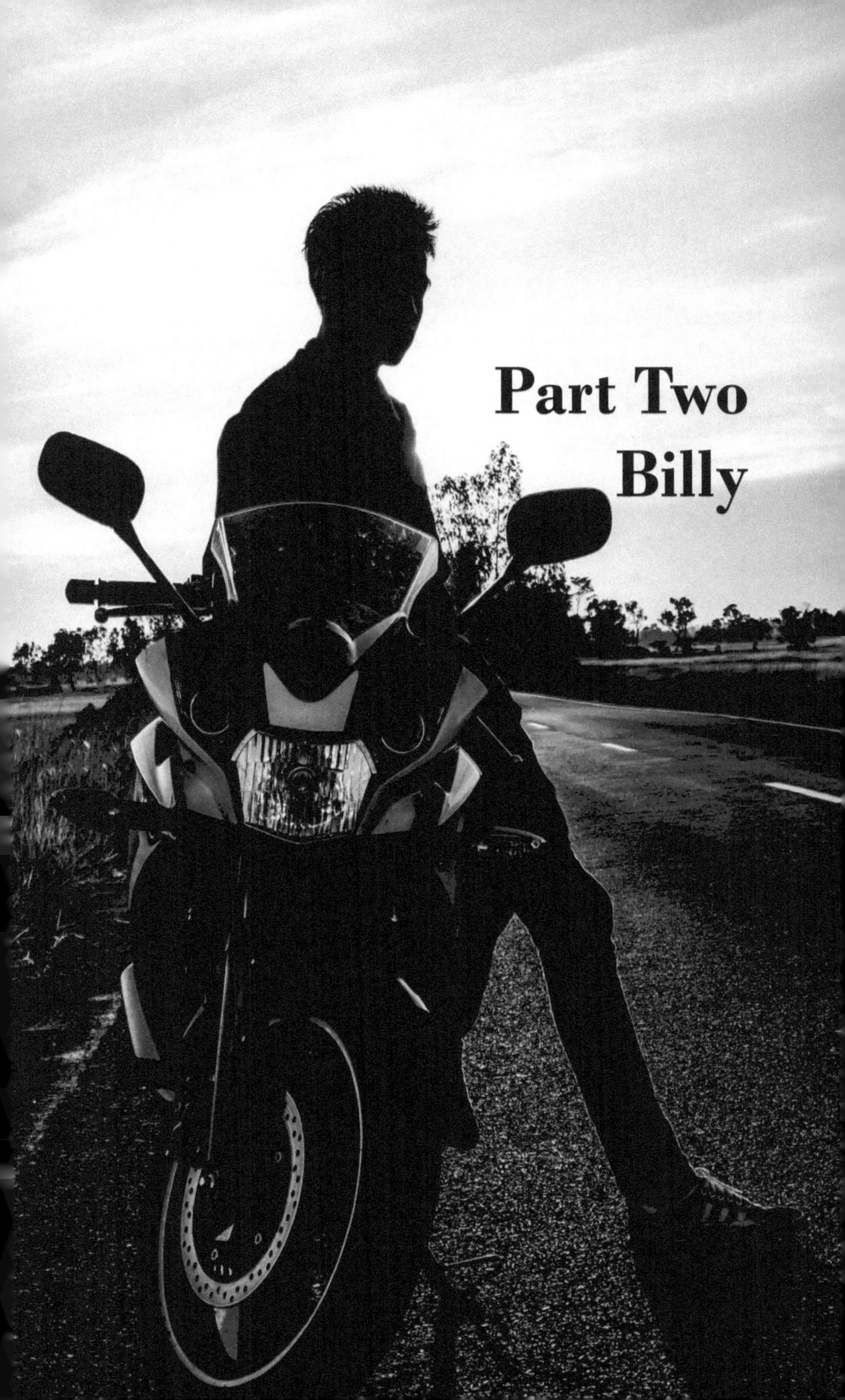

Part Two
Billy

Chapter Eleven

Watching Clara step off the bus to relive her last few hours reminded me of my own death. Like Clara, I didn't want to believe I'd died. And why should I? I had plans for my future. I intended to go to college, maybe study medicine, maybe work abroad and do something worthwhile with my life. Just because I was a biker didn't mean I wanted to be a bum. Most of all, I wanted to marry my girl.

With no limits to what I could imagine, I drove my hog at insane speeds and crashed it repeatedly in hopes that somehow, I would wake up. My anger at death was visceral.

Creating another probable reality was my only hope, and even though I knew it would be difficult and the odds of success slim, I had to do it. I had to take the chance. The odds were worth it.

When I was alive, I always got what I wanted: marks, good looks, the prettiest girl, and the fastest hog. So, why wouldn't lady luck be on my side? Well, she kicked my ass big time, and I made the same mistakes all over again. Making those mistakes a second time woke me up. You see, I'd been wandering around in a half-sleep all my life. The truth is most people do, until something like a tragedy wakes them up.

I hoped Clara's experience would be different, but I had my doubts. If she failed, she was just stubborn enough to end up being the ghost of 32nd street, waiting for the bus for eternity. Reliving her last few hours wouldn't be easy. Every moment would feel as real as if she were experiencing it for the first time, the day she died, Friday, May 12th at 4:32 pm.

That morning, her alarm clock didn't go off, and her favorite music station didn't pull her awake like it usually did on school days. Instead, she felt Lucy pulling on her arm and heard her singing, "It's time to get up. It's time to get up. It's time to get up in the morning."

Clara grunted, lifted her head off the pillow, and dropped it back down again. Trying to awaken from the realm between life and death is like trying to resurface after a fifty-foot dive into deep water.

"Leave me alone. It's Saturday." Her pillow muffled her words.

Lucy pulled the pillow away and hit Clara on the head with it. "It's Friday. Wake up! You're going to be late for school. Quit acting like you're dead or something."

Clara's eyes flickered half-open and shut again. "What time is it?"

Lucy stuck the digital bedside clock under Clara's nose. It read 7:03. After pushing the clock out of her face, Clara hid under the quilt. "It's still early. Leave me alone."

Lucy tugged the quilt away from Clara's face. "I'm not going away. I want to talk to you about something."

"Not now. I'm tired." Clara snuggled back under the covers.

Lucy lifted a corner of the quilt and whispered, "It's about something Isabel said about you."

Mentioning Isabel should have made Clara bolt upright in bed, but not today. She hunkered deeper into the blankets. "If you don't go away, I'm going to hit you. Let me sleep. I have a spare first block."

Lucy sat on the edge of the bed and poked Clara's shoulder, and, when she didn't get a response, pulled on her foot. Clara kicked beneath the covers and yelled, "Go away."

"I can't. Mom said to wake you. She wants to talk to you before she goes to work. You're in big trouble for coming home so late last night." Lucy opened Clara's top dresser drawer.

Clara rolled down the blanket and sat up. She dangled her legs over the bedside. "What are you doing?"

"I'm looking for something."

"Looking for what?" Clara kicked her sister in the butt. "Get out of my stuff." When that didn't stop Lucy, Clara jumped out of bed and slammed the dresser drawer shut. It was then that she saw me in her mirror. She gasped and spun around.

"What are you looking at?" Lucy asked.

"I don't know. I thought I saw someone standing by the window."

Lucy glanced my way. "See who?"

"A man… a man standing in the light." Clara's voice shook. "He's gone now." She flopped back onto the bed. "God, I'm tired."

I hadn't meant to scare her, but I did hope she could see me. I wanted her to know, on some level, she wasn't alone on her last day. Many people do become aware of someone waiting for them when their time is coming to an end.

"Maybe he's your guardian angel," Lucy said.

"Right, like there really is such a thing." Clara sat cross-legged on the bed. "Besides, if I had a guardian angel, everything in my life would be perfect, and right now, it isn't. And he certainly wouldn't look like that guy."

Hey, that hurt my feelings.

"What did he look like?" Lucy opened Clara's jewelry box, and a tiny ballerina in a pink tutu twirled on pointe to a tinny rendition of a Chopin waltz. Lucy took an amber cabochon on a silver chain from the box.

"You're not wearing my necklace," Clara swung her legs over the bed, grabbed the pendant out of Lucy's hand, dropped it into the jewelry box, and slammed the lid shut. "He looked like a biker."

"Cool. If I had a guardian angel, I'd want him to look like a biker. Send him over to me."

Clara sat on the edge of the bed and held her head in her hands. "I have a splitting headache."

"Were you drinking last night? You're acting like you have a hangover."

"Like you know what a hangover feels like."

Lucy opened the music box again, and the ballerina spun slower, this time with the music becoming a series of pings. "Ugh, I hate this dancing doll. She's so annoying."

I had to agree. The music box rendition of one of Chopin's waltzes grated on my nerves worse than fingernails scraping across the blackboard. Lucy picked up a silver-wrapped crystal hanging from a leather cord. She clasped the necklace around her neck and admired it in the mirror. "I've seen Daddy with a hangover, and Janie and I drank some stuff at her place when I went for a sleepover. Boy, did I puke a lot."

"It pisses me off. You never get caught for the bad things you do, and I spend a little extra time with Peter, and I'm in trouble." Clara yanked the music box out from underneath Lucy's hands just as she began to rummage through Clara's tangled mess of earrings.

"Mom thinks Peter is a bad influence on you. She thinks you're getting way too serious. Are you?" Lucy picked up a tube of lipstick, a mauve color, and applied it to her lips. I was surprised that Clara didn't try to stop her. I suspect this was par for the course when dealing with a younger sister. I was just as bad with my older brother. I borrowed his clothes, especially socks, as I never seemed to have matching pairs. Lucy dabbed the corners of her mouth with a tissue while watching Clara's reaction in the mirror.

"So, what if we are? What about you and Tommy?" Clara walked toward the window where I stood watching. I didn't think Clara could see me. At least I hoped she couldn't. I moved and stood by the door and was relieved when Clara didn't turn my way. Still, I couldn't help but think that she sensed my presence.

"This isn't about Tommy and me," Lucy said. "Besides, Mom still thinks I'm too young to get into too much trouble. It's one of the advantages of being the youngest, you know.

"Don't I know it," Clara said. "Parents practice on their first child and get it right with their second."

I'd have to disagree with Clara on that one. It's true. My parents were a lot harder on my older brother. Too hard. But sometimes, I'd wished they took more notice of what I was doing. Yeah, maybe if they did, I wouldn't be dead. Not that I am blaming them or anything.

"So, I'm just warning you. Mom's mad that you didn't call last night." Lucy opened the bottom dresser drawer and took out a sweater.

"Hey, I'm wearing that sweater today," Clara said through a series of yawns.

Lucy slipped the sweater over her tank top.

"You thief." Clara grabbed the hem, but Lucy crossed her arms in front of her chest so Clara couldn't lift the sweater over her head. "I need to wear my sweater today. It's my good luck sweater, and I have an audition. I want my necklace too."

"I don't have anything else to wear, and I need to look good, and I don't want to look like a geek. You know how nasty some of the girls are. I hate it when they make fun of my outfit."

"Take it off."

"I don't want to be a mark, like Cindy. You've seen the way she dresses. God, I wouldn't be caught dead in some of her clothes. People say she's not all there, you know, kind of crazy."

"She's not crazy." Clara pulled her slippers out from under the bed. "Who's saying this?"

"Your so-called friends. I hear them talk shit about you behind your back."

"Like what?"

"Like… I don't know. Things. You're not good enough for Peter."

"I don't want to hear this."

"I don't think he likes you anymore. I saw him kissing Isabel."

"When?"

"Yesterday."

"No way you didn't. Peter wouldn't do that. Whatever they had together is over now."

"I know what I saw. Ask him about it. He'll probably lie."

"I will. Now, get out of my room. I need to get dressed and

meet Peter at the coffee shop. He wants to buy me a birthday breakfast. Did you even remember?"

"Yeah, I did. Happy birthday."

"That was heartfelt."

Lucy picked lint from the sweater. "It's just that…I don't know. You'd better watch your back too. Now that you're hanging with Cindy. It's bad for your reputation. People think differently about you now."

"I don't care what they think of me. Now give me back my sweater?" Clara tugged on the sleeve.

Lucy raced from the room. A moment later, the front door slammed. Clara lay back on her bed and looked at the ceiling where a fly thrashed inside the light fixture. "I'm sixteen today," she said to no one but the fly and me. "And I can't wait until I'm seventeen."

A knock startled her into sitting upright. She looked at her bedside clock. 7:17 am. "Shit," she said under her breath.

"Clara, can I come in?" Marie's voice hadn't changed in all these years. It still had that same effect on me, like butter toffee, smooth, sweet, and always leaving me wanting more.

"I'm awake." Clara slipped out of bed and opened her closet door. A mound of dirty clothes covered the floor. "Damn Lucy, I wanted to wear that sweater. Now, what am I going to wear?"

Marie opened the door. Clara spun around and growled, "I'll be down in a minute."

Marie's hair, shorter than when I knew her, was parted to the side with loose curls that touched her shoulders. Her eyes, a stormy blue, were lined with worry. Her sleeveless sundress accented her slim waistline and fell short enough to reveal her elegant legs. The sun caught her ring. My ring. I'd picked it out myself. It was all I could do to scrounge enough money from odd jobs like working in a warehouse, graveyard hours at the gas station, and the odd bit of construction work, usually ditch digging. When I still didn't have enough money, I sold one of my favorite hogs. The love you feel for someone special never goes away, not even after death.

Marie sat on the edge of the bed. "We need to talk." I'd heard that tone of voice before. It always made my stomach flop. It meant I'd hurt her in some way.

"Yeah, I know. Lucy told me." Clara rifled through her clothes. She complained the grey sweater made her look fat, the tweed one made her look frumpy, and the cashmere one had too many pills.

Marie tried to help her. She suggested several items hanging in the closet above Clara's head.

"I don't like any of those clothes," Clara said. "That's why they are still on hangers."

"Why not give them to Lucy?"

"Lucy won't wear out-of-style clothes. Hell, she's always stealing my best clothes for herself. She took the sweater I was going to wear today." Clara rolled a t-shirt into a ball and dropped it onto the heap of clothes in the closet. "All my favorite things are dirty." She smelt the underarms of a green and yellow batik blouse. "I guess I could wear this." She hung it over the back of the desk chair.

"It's your responsibility to get your clothes into the wash. I'm not going to do that for you anymore. By the way, Happy Birthday."

"Don't forget. You promised nothing special. No surprises."

"It's your sixteenth. It's a special birthday. Did you at least invite the girls over for a sleepover tonight?"

"No. I have my audition, and Peter and I are going out after."

So, Marie didn't know Clara was having trouble with her friends. Not unusual, I guess. Now that I think about it, I didn't tell my parents everything. If they didn't ask, why worry them, was my motto.

Marie crossed her arms. "Where did you go last night? You didn't answer your cell."

"I turned it off at school and forgot to turn it back on. I didn't get your messages until I came home and found you sleeping on the couch. I didn't want to wake you."

"I called Peter's cellphone too."

"Mom, I'm sorry. I should have called you, okay?"

"Why didn't you?" Marie said.

Watch out, Clara. I never won an argument with Marie.

"I don't know. I guess I didn't want you to tell me to come home. I wanted to stay out with Peter."

"You never go out with the girls anymore."

"Ashley and I aren't talking to each other right now, and Isabel has never been a true friend, and Tina is well, what can I say about that piece of trash."

Marie frowned. "No one deserves to be called that. It isn't like you to be so unkind."

Clara leaned against her closet door. "You're right. I'm sorry, sort of."

"Either you're sorry, or you're not."

"I'm not."

"I'm sad for you. There's nothing like a girlfriend you can trust."

"Yeah, well, I can't trust any of them anymore."

"Why not invite Cindy?"

"Right, like I'd really do that. She's part of the reason no one has anything to do with me anymore. I try to do the right thing, and it backfires. It's all about who you hang with, you know."

"Lucy said that you and Cindy were becoming close friends."

"Hardly. I wonder where Lucy got that idea. I've been helping Cindy with her schoolwork and walking home with her. That's all."

"It's nice of you to do that."

"Right, like I'm in the running for sainthood because of it."

"Clara…"

"I know. I hate myself for thinking it, but Cindy isn't my friend. We don't have the same interests. We hardly know what to talk about." Clara pulled the elastic out of her ponytail. "Let's just do a family thing this weekend. When I turn seventeen, we'll have a big party, okay? I have my audition tonight anyway, and that's all I want to think about right now."

Marie looked tired. I wanted to put my arms around her. She brushed a strand of hair from her eyes. "I need to get to work, and if you don't hurry, you'll be late for school."

"Mom, will you write me a note? I have a headache, and I need to take the morning off."

"Your birthday is not an excuse for skipping school."

"I have first block free anyway, and all I would miss would be the band class. I'll get detention if I don't have a note, and I have my audition after school. I can't miss it. Please."

Marie had a faraway look in her eye. She wanted to be an actress once. Like Clara, Marie was a triple threat. She could sing, dance, and act better than any other girl at the school. I wasn't bad myself and, when we both won the leads in the school musical *Grease,* we fell in love. But children have a way of changing your dreams, and so does death.

"If you go to band practice, you won't need a note. Besides, it's your own fault you have a headache. You know the rules, school nights in by nine o'clock. I don't even know what time you came home. It had to be after eleven. I tried to stay awake, but I fell asleep after I phoned Peter."

It was after midnight, but Clara wasn't going to admit it. After going to a movie, they decided to walk by the river, where they sat on a log and made out. She couldn't tell Marie that. I don't blame her. I wouldn't have told my mom I was making out at that age.

"Please," Clara tried again. "It's my birthday."

"Clara, I know how much you like Peter, but…what's this?" She touched the hickey on Clara's neck.

Clara pushed her hand away. "This isn't about Peter. All I want is a note."

Marie looked at her watch. "I haven't time for this. It's 7:25. I'm going to be late for work."

"The note?"

"No."

Clara stomped out of the bedroom. It was close to eight o'clock by the time she showered and dressed. She sat at Marie's writing desk and rummaged around the drawer, and found my pocket watch. She puzzled over it for a moment running her thumb over the etching of the motorcycle. "What's this doing here?" She pressed it to her ear and listened to the ticking. My heart warmed to think Marie had the watch repaired and kept it set and running all these years. Clara opened the lid and read the inscription aloud. *To Billy. All my love, Marie.*

"Billy? Who's Billy?" After she snapped it closed, she placed the watch back in the drawer and searched for a pen, one that still had ink in it. She wrote a note excusing herself from morning classes and signed Marie's name. It was an excellent forgery.

Chapter Twelve

I waited for Clara in front of the coffee shop where I'd set up to do a little busking and a lot of eavesdropping. I loved the bustle of people with newspapers under their arms, coming and going from the café, chatting on cellphones, and sipping espresso from paper cups. The smell of coffee, just seeing it brought the memories back in a mouthwatering wave of longing. I loved coffee, black as mechanic's grease, and fresh-cut fries smothered in ketchup and dripping with vinegar. Back when I hung out at the café, it was a burger joint. In those days, the café became a hangout for the local bikers and some gangs. It had changed so much I hardly recognized the place. The new owners had added an outside patio covered with an awning. Planters filled with red geraniums and white star flowers gave our old dive a little class.

Peter sat outside on the patio. He drummed his fingers against the tabletop in time to my music while he waited for Clara. He looked at his watch every few minutes. As time went on, his drumming became more intense. Clara had an issue with time, and it annoyed him. I think he was worried she might stand him up.

From where I stood, I could see her get off the bus and make her way toward the café. She didn't dawdle, but she didn't hurry either. Once, she stopped to admire something in a storefront window. When she walked by me, she stopped to listen to me play. It may have been wishful thinking on my part, but I thought I saw a flicker of recognition in her eyes before she dropped some coins into my clarinet case. Not quite a dollar, ninety-five cents. I performed an extra-special flourish of notes on my clarinet and nodded my thanks.

"Hey," she hung her bag over a chair and slipped into a seat next to Peter.

He pushed a latte toward her. "Here, it's getting cold." He looked at his watch. "After last night, I thought you might not come."

"Oh, c'mon, I'm only ten minutes late," she said.

"Twelve minutes." He tapped the face of his watch.

"Did you miss me that much?"

"More."

She wrapped both hands around the cup and took a sip. "It's perfect. Thank you." Peter wiped the line of foam from her upper lip with his finger. There was a split second where I thought he might kiss her. The moment was ripe. Their auras shone with passion. If it were me, I would have gone in for the kiss, but Clara sabotaged the moment when she fingered a button on his shirt.

"Well…um. You, okay?" Peter put a finger under her chin and lifted her head so she would look him in the eyes. She didn't. Her eyes stayed fixated on his button.

"Happy birthday." Peter leaned over and kissed the top of her head. When she didn't respond, his hand hovered over the donuts before choosing a glazed chocolate donut covered in sprinkles and pressed it to her lips. She took a bite, closed her eyes, and made a sound like a cross between a purr and a bliss-filled groan. It did look good.

He placed a bubble-wrapped parcel in front of her. "Sorry, but I didn't have time to wrap it."

In truth, he bought the kaleidoscope from me twenty minutes before Clara arrived at the cafe. To make my disguise look realistic, I placed a few items to sell on the ground in front of me—small trinkets made from pieces of glass, silver, and gemstones. I made the kaleidoscope for Clara in both realities. I hoped Peter would buy it for her birthday and he did both times.

"Thank you. You're so sweet." She kissed him, and he took the opportunity to lick the chocolate from her lips.

"Open it," he said. "But be careful because it's more fragile than it looks.

She peeled the tape off the bubble wrap and rolled out a kaleidoscope.

"Oh, it's beautiful and so unique. I've never seen a kaleidoscope like this before. Lucy and I had one when we were young, a plastic tube with tiny pieces of glitter inside. But his Kaleidoscope is a work of art. Thank you." She leaned over and kissed him. They lingered for a moment, kissing a second time. Young love. I felt the stirrings of what I had with Marie. The love and the loss all came rushing back to me as I watched the two looking into each other's eyes, eyes that said so much when lips said nothing.

Don't get me wrong. I'm a happy spook and very good at my job. Not many have my talents, and not many can manifest their physical form. Still, now and then, I miss the touch of soft hands and the warmth of two shoulders pressed together as one. For a moment, I almost wished I were sixteen again, almost.

Clara placed the kaleidoscope over one eye and looked through it. "Where did you find it?"

"A street vendor." Peter looked at me and gave me a thumbs up. My cue to play the Beetles song, "When I'm Sixty-four." It's an oldie, but Peter thought it would be funny for me to play it for Clara on her birthday. It's one of those songs that suits the clarinet, and I gave it as much schmaltz as I could muster. She sang along and at one point stood to dance through a verse while Peter stayed seated but holding her hand. When I'd finished the song, she sat in his lap and kissed him. I pulled my clarinet into sections and pretended to wipe it out so I could listen to them talk.

"I hope we're still together when I'm sixty-four," he took her hand and played with her fingers.

"You never know, I might not live to sixty-four," she said.

Peter frowned. "Don't say that."

"Ah, look at you being so serious. I was teasing you." She kissed the tip of his nose.

"That's not funny." He hung his head and looked at his hands resting in his lap. "My mom was only thirty-eight."

I felt sorry for the kid. If Clara failed to change the course of events, her death would be a double whammy.

"Oh, I'm so sorry. I'd forgotten. Stupid me. Stupid joke. I only said it because my grandma died at sixty-two. She didn't make sixty-four, and neither did my grandpa. I think she died of a broken heart."

"Well, don't go and break mine. I don't think I could take it." Peter downed the rest of his latte in one gulp.

"Or you break mine."

"I'd never do that." He brushed his hand through her hair. She pulled away and sat back with a sullen expression. You would have thought a storm cloud had blown in and darkened the café.

Clara looked my way, partially to avoid Peter's eyes and partly because she became aware of me watching and listening to them. I faked almost dropping my mouthpiece. I adjusted the reed and played a few notes making sure it squeaked so I had an excuse to take it off again, which I did.

Peter twirled the kaleidoscope's wheels. "What's wrong?" he asked.

"Oh, I don't know. Something Lucy said."

"About me?"

"Yeah."

"Hey, we don't keep secrets."

"Don't we?" You could have chilled a bottle of wine with her look.

"Lay it on me."

"She said she saw you kissing Isabel."

Peter sat back in his chair and took a deep breath. I'd made the same mistake once and lived to regret it. Marie had caught me kissing a biker gal I'd met one night at the burger joint. Marie and I had a falling out, so I thought, what the hell. Big mistake. My stomach tightened as I recalled the kiss. Peter would feel like shit right now, and rightly so. I'd almost lost Marie that day, and Peter was close to losing Clara. What was I thinking? He was going to lose her forever.

Peter gripped the table. "She did see us kiss, but it's not what you think."

"I know what a kiss means."

"No, listen. Isabel kissed me. I didn't kiss her."

"C'mon, Peter. Get real."

"No, really. Isabel pulled me into a kiss when Lucy came by, so she would say something to you and make you jealous."

Clara picked the sprinkles off her half-eaten donut. "I guess I can see Isabel doing that but …but I know how much she still likes you. She thinks I stole you from her, and sometimes when I see you two together, it's like you're still a couple. You know what I mean?"

Peter took her hand in his and licked the sprinkles from her fingers. She pulled her hand away and wiped it on a napkin. On any other day, she may have found his gesture endearing, perhaps romantic, but right now, it grossed her out. "Why didn't you push her away?"

"I didn't have to because the kiss was quick, a peck really, no feeling, nothing… a peck."

"Right. A peck."

"I'm telling you like it is. I don't like Isabel anymore, and thank God Lucy came by because they went off together."

Clara pushed her latte to the center of the table. She turned in her chair to face Peter, who was looking down at his knees. "What business did she have with Lucy?"

"I don't know, but she seemed more interested in talking to Lucy than hanging with me."

Clara banged her hand on the table. Peter jumped, and so did I.

"I don't get it. Why don't you just tell Isabel to leave you alone? She has a hold on you for some reason, and I want to know why."

"It's difficult to explain." He stood and turned to face me. His fear of losing her was too strong for him to tell her the truth.

Clara stood and placed the kaleidoscope into her bag. She held back tears.

Peter placed a hand on her arm. "Where are you going?"

"There is no point sticking around here." She shook his hand off her arm as she backed away from him. "I might as well go to band."

"I thought we were skipping band today. Didn't you get a note?"

"Sort of." She tried to stifle a smile. "I wrote it myself."

"Me too." Peter laughed nervously. "As if my old man would ever do that for me. Hell, he's too self-absorbed to notice if I'm home or have had supper or whatever. I'm invisible at home. You're making me feel invisible now."

"And you're making me feel like I'm not important to you. Like I'm not your girl. You asked me if I would love you when we're sixty-four, but we won't make it if we can't share everything with each other." She pushed him in the chest. "Do you deny that you and Isabel share a secret?" He took her hands in his.

"Yes, I mean no. It's something I can't talk to you about right now, especially not today."

"Why not today?"

"Because it's your sixteenth birthday. All I ask is that you trust me when I say nothing is going on between Isabel and me. Nothing at all."

She pulled her hands away from Peter's. "Trust goes both ways. You have so many secrets. How can I trust you?"

"Look how you're acting. This kind of reaction was what I

was afraid of."

"So, it's that bad?"

"No. It's just…complicated."

"Okay, don't tell me then if keeping a secret is more important than us." Bristling, she spun around and walked out of the café. She wiped tears from her eyes when she walked by me. Peter glanced at his watch—9:41 a.m. He sighed. It was going to be a long day—a long day for all of us.

Chapter Thirteen

I wasn't a straight-A student like Clara, but I did get top marks in band. I loved all kinds of music: folk, rock, blues, jazz, and classical. I took a seat in the clarinet section beside Cindy. While everyone else warmed up their instruments, she drew a picture on the back of a piece of band music, "March to the Gallows" by Hector Berlioz, the fourth movement of his "Symphonie Fantastique." She kept her head down, ignoring the rest of the students as they filed into class. A dissonant wall of sound filled the air: clinking stands, muted trumpets, horns, flutes, and timpani rolls. It was chaos, and I loved it.

Cindy's cut-off jeans were fringed, and her blousy shirt fell to the top of her thighs. Her sleeves, rolled to her elbows, exposed a streak of blue paint on her forearm. Beads of yellow paint dappled her fingernails. Her last class must have been art, as the paint still smelled fresh. Toes painted with a spiral design poked out of her sandals. In my time, I would have liked a girl like Cindy. She had that retro-artsy-hippy thing going on. Yep, she was one cool chick, and for the life of me, I couldn't see why anyone would want to be mean to her. Her red paisley bandana had slid back on her head, allowing a wisp of hair tinged with blue paint to stick straight out. Forgetting myself, I leaned over to touch it, to tuck it in for her. With eyes owl-wide, she looked at me. My electromagnetic heart leaped into my throat. I pulled my hand away. Surely, she couldn't see me. Could she? I breathed easier when she resumed sketching on the back of the music. I looked over her shoulder to see her artwork, and for the second time, in less than a minute, my heart skipped a beat. She was drawing a person, a man, and that man was me. The likeness was uncanny. It rattled me, and I blinked out of my physical form and back again.

During Clara's last day, I hadn't sat with Cindy in the clarinet section. I hadn't related to her at all. In fact, I didn't know anything about her. This time, for some reason, I felt drawn to her. Her sensitivity fascinated me. Her envelope of sadness overwhelmed me. I had warned Clara how easy it was to change the course of things. I, too, would have to be careful. With one small gesture, I could turn events upside-down.

Clara walked into the band room and sat in my chair. I slid away so she could have it all to herself.

"Hey, who's that?" Clara pointed to my picture sitting on Cindy's music stand. "He looks familiar." I detected a slight tremble in her voice.

"Don't you know?" Cindy took the piece of music, turned it face up, and placed it on her stand.

"No. Do you care to tell me?" Clara said.

"Not really. You wouldn't believe me."

"Try me."

"He's a ghost."

"Okay, if you don't want to tell me." Clara shrugged and went to sit in the flute section but just as she was going to sit, Peter, who played trombone, slid his slide out as far as it would go and hit her bottom as she sat. Some of the trombone players laughed, and one trumpeter played a muted wow, wow, wow.

Clara turned around and glared at Peter. "That's not funny."

He gave her a puppy-dog smile. She turned away and took her flute from the case, and put it together.

Peter tried again to get her attention with his trombone, this time catching a strand of her hair with the spit valve. Clara whipped around, grabbed the slide, and pulled it out. Peter reached for the slide, but Clara held it in the air out of reach. "You do that again, and I'm going to bend it."

"Holy shit, don't bend it." Peter paled. "I'm screwed if you wreck it. You know I can't afford to get it fixed. Give it to me."

"What will you give me for it?"

This playful turn of events surprised me as I thought she was still angry at him. Women were unpredictable, and I still had a hard time second-guessing them.

Peter raised his arms wide. "Anything you want."

Clara looked over at the saxophone section. Isabel was watching her. "A kiss."

No one was more surprised than me at Clara's request except Peter, who raised an eyebrow. "In class?"

"Yeah. You have a problem with that?"

"Hell no." He brushed her hair back from her face, leaned over, and kissed her. The girls in the flute section counted the seconds like bars of music—one, two, three, four, two, two, three, four. A trumpeter played his muted wow, wow, wow again. Clara blushed and whispered in Peter's ear. "You upset me, you know."

"Really? I didn't notice." He flashed his cutest smile again. "Hey, meet me at lunch. We'll talk."

"Did you see that?" Tina said. She and Isabel were sitting behind me in the saxophone section.

"See what?" Isabel asked.

"Peter and Clara kissing right here in class."

"Yeah, I saw them," Isabel said. "I hate her."

"Never mind her. Look what I made." Tina removed a necklace from under her cardigan and dangled it in front of Isabel. The chain was strung with beads interspersed with dried crickets—a gruesome attempt at creative self-expression.

Isabel leaned as far back in her chair as possible. "That's sick, but I love it," she said with a sly smile.

"And I have this," Tina pulled a glass jar from her bag and screwed off the cap. The crickets crawled over each other as they tried to climb the sides of the jar to escape.

Isabel pursed her lips. "Hurry, put the lid on before they get out."

"You're not scared of them, are you?" Tina pushed the jar under Isabel's nose. Isabel slapped the jar away, almost knocking it out of Tina's hands.

"You know I hate bugs," Isabel shrieked. She was on the verge of a panic attack. So now I knew Isabel had a weakness—a bug phobia. I wondered if Clara knew.

Tina screwed the lid back on the jar. "I love bugs. Do you think Cindy likes bugs as much as I do?"

"Probably does," Isabel said. "I'm sure her house is full of them. She probably sleeps with them too."

I'd been the brunt of my friends' jokes from time to time, but I never experienced the isolation and meanness Cindy endured every day. Tina opened the jar and let a cricket crawl onto her index nail, a red spike. All she had to do was flick it, and it fell onto Cindy's shoulder, where it proceeded to crawl down Cindy's neck and into her blouse.

If ever I wished I weren't a spook, it was today. But what could I do but watch and listen to their cruel laughter blended with the cacophony of notes splayed across the room like random bullets? I could see the bug's shadow crawling down Cindy's back and her shoulder blade rippling in response. It tumbled out from under her blouse and fell underneath her chair.

A moment later, Mr. Bradley, the band teacher, entered the room. Just like magic, all the sound stopped when he stepped onto the conductor's podium. He motioned for Ashley, the oboe player, to tune everyone individually. When my turn came, I let my note ring through the room. Cindy looked at me again and smiled. I almost spoke to her, but she had enough problems and didn't need her classmates to see her talking to invisible people. They already had her pegged as nuts, and I wouldn't be helping her out by my meddling. When Tina tried to tune her sax, I ensured that all she could play was a squeak. Isabel too. They both kept trying, but the squawking was worse than two seagulls fighting over a French fry. The more they tried, the louder the students laughed. Mr. Bradley wasn't amused. He told Tina that if she were ever going to play with good technique, she would have to cut her nails.

"That's not going to happen," she said through her reed-filled mouth. "I'd rather fail music than cut my nails." She bit down on the mouthpiece and squeaked again. Mr. Bradly winced and told her to change the reed. I knew better than to meddle, but I had to do something, so I decided that a little harmless intervention on Cindy's behalf would be okay. I made sure a new reed gave her grief too.

"Now everyone will find a new piece of music on their stands," Mr. Bradley said. "It's a transcription of Beethoven's Ninth Symphony. His last complete symphony. Some of you may recognize the theme, "Ode to Joy.""

The first clarinet's hand shot up. "Why did so many composers die after finishing their ninth symphony? Is there really such a thing as the curse of the ninth?"

"There is," Clara said, putting her hand up and speaking at the same time. "It's because nine is the final number. That's why they say cats have nine lives. Nine signifies the ultimate attainment, so when the composers completed their highest possible goal, they died."

"That's just crazy," Ashley said, blowing spit from one of the oboe's keys. "Numerology is a form of superstition. Superstitious people are in denial." Ashley rolled her eyes and sucked on her oboe reed.

"What about Bach?" Clara said. "His music is filled with numerology. In fact, music is just a form of audible numbers. Right?"

"I hear colors," Cindy said.

I winced. It was a brave thing to say, but I wished Cindy had kept that fact to herself. Confessing she could hear colors was sure to get her into trouble.

"That's why you're so good at art," Mr. Bradley said.

I was thankful for his kindness and his quick interjection before someone could say something nasty to her.

He raised his baton, and the clarinets began the main theme in unison. I was surprised when I heard Cindy play. Her playing was far superior to the first clarinetist's tone and tuning, yet she sat with the third clarinets. I smiled at the squawking in the saxophone section behind me.

After music class, Tina dropped the remaining crickets down Cindy's shirt as she leaned over to put her instrument away. Cindy's backbone rippled beneath her blouse. She stood and reached her hand behind her back and scratched like crazy. A cricket crawled from under her blouse to the hem where it hung upside down. When Cindy saw the bug, she flicked it off. Two more crickets dropped to the floor. Cindy spun in a circle, now aware that more crickets were dropping out of her blouse. Frantic, she raised her blouse above her belly button, pierced with a delicate bird charm. A cricket crisscrossed her stomach. Swallowing a cry, she dashed out of the band room. I debated whether I should follow her into the lady's room. I did. Clara followed me.

"Cindy, what's wrong," she asked and knelt to look under Cindy's stall.

"Tina," Cindy said. "She dropped crickets down my blouse."

Two crickets dropped to the floor. They were still alive and began to crawl toward Clara, who scooped them up and dropped them out the bathroom window.

The toilet flushed. A moment later, Cindy came out of the stall.

"We can't let her get away with this," Clara said. "We have to get her back."

"How?" Cindy fluffed out her blouse and dislodged a cricket still caught in the folds of the fabric.

"Aren't you working in the cafeteria today?" Clara asked. The devious sparkle in her eyes reminded me of Marie's when she was up to no good. And truth be told, Marie was every much a rebel as Clara. That's why she chose me as her boyfriend. I was wild. I was fun. I lived my life on the edge as if every moment were my last.

Cindy nodded. "Yes, but I don't see how that will help us get her back."

"What's the lunch special today?"

"Grilled cheese."

"Perfect. Tina always orders the grilled cheese. It's her favorite. And if we plan it right, we can turn her lunch into a nightmare. C'mon."

"Where?"

"The biology room. It's my turn to feed the bearded dragon. But we'll have to hurry."

I had a bad feeling about what Clara was planning. I had a beardy once, a red beauty. Her name was Rosie, and if ever a man loved a dog, I loved my bearded dragon as my best friend. Now, I knew where Tina found the crickets. I suspected Clara was going after the mealworms.

Chapter Fourteen

The lunch line snaked from the cafeteria into the hallway. No wonder. The daily specials were pizza and grilled cheese sandwiches with fries, not chili and wieners or meatloaf and veggies like in my day. Isabel, Ashley, and Tina struck up a conversation with some guys near the front of the line and slyly positioned themselves beside them. The guys didn't mind having the girls' attention, but some students behind them grumbled among themselves about the girls butting in. No one challenged the trio, though.

Cindy placed three sandwiches to the side of her tray. She prepared them ahead of time in case Isabel, Tina and Ashley ordered the grilled cheese. When they came through her station, she didn't look up at them, but I saw a quirky smile forming on her lips. The girls were too busy flirting with the guys to give Cindy a moment's notice. The only glitch happened when Ashley almost ordered pizza instead of grilled cheese. At the last minute, she changed her mind.

After Cindy served them, she took off her apron and went to talk to her supervisor, who excused Cindy from cafeteria duty as Cindy feigned sickness.

Peter placed his lunch tray on the table and slid into a seat beside Clara. She didn't look up or say hello. Nothing was going to break her focus on the meal line. She had an untouched Greek salad in front of her.

"Are you still mad at me?" He leaned his shoulder into hers. A feeble smile told me she was still troubled. He stole a cucumber from her salad and popped it in his mouth. "I'm sorry. Sometimes I'm a jerk."

"You really are." She pushed her salad in front of him. "Take it. I'm not hungry anyway." He pushed it back. "If you like, we can talk after school."

"I have my audition after school."

"Right. What time?"

"Five-thirty. Downtown at the Centennial Theatre."

"I'll come with you. How about I meet you at the bus stop at four-fifteen? After your audition, we can go and get a bite to eat and talk. I'll tell you what's been going on. Okay?" He picked up his grilled cheese and held it to her lips. "C'mon. Take a bite. You need your strength for your audition." At the sight of the sandwich, her face tuned birch-tree-white.

Clara snatched the grilled cheese out of his hand and pulled the bread apart from the cheese.

"Hey, take a bite, don't maul it," he said.

"I had to see if—"

"See what?" Peter ate a fry and offered her one.

She shook her head. She folded the sandwich back together and gave it to him. "It's okay."

"Why wouldn't it be? Did someone spit on it or something?"

"No…but they may have put something inside it."

"Like what?"

Clara shrugged and waved Cindy over, who had just come into the cafeteria. She sat beside Clara and whispered. "Did I miss anything?"

"Not yet. The girls are too busy flirting with the guys," Clara said.

If there is anything that will stop a girl from eating, it is a guy's attention. After all, you can't look glamorous with lettuce stuck between your teeth. Tina picked up her sandwich three times to take a bite, but she laid it back on her plate every time a boy turned to say something to her. Clara groaned every time it happened. So did I. We were all on the edge of our seats. I'd never eaten a cheese and mealworm sandwich, but I could imagine the taste. It gave me the willies to think about it.

"Hey, what's up?" Marty said as he took a seat beside Cindy. Marty opened a brown lunch bag and took out two ham and cheese sandwiches. He offered one to Cindy, who waved it away with a sick look on her face.

"Watch them," Cindy said, looking in the direction of the three girls.

Marty leaned over Cindy to ask Peter. "What's going on?"

"Beats me," Peter said. "Something to do with the three witches of Woodland High."

Clara smiled. "Is that what you call them?"

"When I'm being nice." Peter offered her another french-fry, but she pushed his hand away. "So why are we watching them?"

"Wait and see," Clara said.

Every time Tina picked up her sandwich, my stomach jumped

into my throat. When Tina finally took a big bite, my stomach, as insubstantial as it was, heaved. Tina took a second mouthful, chewed, frowned, and stopped chewing. She covered her mouth with her hand. I could tell she wanted to spit it out, but everyone was looking at her, including Clara and Cindy, whose jaws had dropped. Somehow, Tina managed to swallow. I saw the lump of bread, mealworms, and cheese go down her esophagus.

"Oh gross." Clara clutched her stomach.

"What's wrong?" Isabel asked Tina, who turned a sickly shade of grey.

Tina downed the remainder of her pop in one gulp. "It tastes bad. Don't eat yours."

Isabel peeled Tina's sandwich apart. Mealworms dangled from strings of melted cheese. Tina gagged and vomited all over the table. Everyone pulled back, knocking over chairs to get away from the mess.

Pop spewed from Tina's nose as she ran from the cafeteria. The shock on everyone's faces would have been hilarious if not for the stench of vomit. Everyone scrambled to clear the room as both Isabel and Ashley pried open their sandwiches. Ashley dropped hers on the table and held a hand to her mouth. It was crawling with mealworms.

"Nasty." Peter pulled his t-shirt over his nose. "I'm out of here. I have practice at noon. See you later?"

Clara grabbed his hand to keep him from leaving. "Meet me at the bus stop," she said. There was something about the way her fingers slipped through his as he turned to leave that made her frown. I wondered if unconsciously she knew that it would be the last time she would hold his hand.

Marty looked inside his sandwich. "What was in it?"

"Mealworms." Clara buried her nose in the sleeve of her blouse. "Not yours. You brought your sandwich from home. They're in Tina's."

"Not just Tina's," Cindy explained. "In Ashley's and Isabel's sandwiches too. All three ordered grilled cheese today."

Marty covered his mouth with his hand. "Oh God, you did that? They're gonna kill you."

Cindy pinched her nose. "I did, and I'm not sorry. It was Clara's idea. They dropped live crickets down my blouse when we were in band class."

"There'll be hell to pay, and here it comes," Marty said as they watched Isabel weave her way between the tables and chairs. Her eyes were like granite.

"You did this, didn't you?" she hissed and dropped her sandwich open-faced in front of Cindy.

"Did what?" Cindy kept her eyes averted.

"The hell, you know. When I tell, you'll lose your job and your free lunch."

"If you tell, I'll tell what you've been doing to me. You'll be expelled," Cindy pushed back her chair and stood.

"No one will believe you."

"I believe her." Clara stood and faced Isabel. "And for the record, it was my idea."

Isabel's eyes narrowed. "I should have known. You're gonna pay for this. You both will." Isabel took the sandwich and smacked it against Clara's chest.

Clara gagged. A dry gag as she hadn't eaten since breakfast. She shook the mealworms from her shirt.

Marty stood and gripped Isabel's arm. "Hey, that's not cool."

She shook him off. "Get your hands off me, nerd. Let's go, Ashley. I can't stand looking at these losers."

Ashley held back until Isabel cleared the cafeteria door. "She won't let this go, you know." She hugged her stomach. "I feel uh…" She turned and ran to catch up with Isabel.

Cindy picked mealworms from the folds of Clara's blouse. "This has been the best day. Did you see Tina's face? Her eyes were bugged out. I've never seen anything so funny. It feels so good to get them back, and I would never have done anything like this without you. I wouldn't have had the nerve. Thank you for helping me."

"Watch your back, both of you." Marty stuffed the last bite of his sandwich into his mouth.

Like Marty, I had a feeling this was going to turn out bad.

"We have to stick together," Clara said. "Especially before and after school. Marty, could you walk Cindy home today? I can't as I have an audition."

Cindy blushed, but Marty, oblivious to the crush she had on him, said, "Sure. No worries. I can do that."

Clara pulled the blouse over her head, and when her black tank top rose with the blouse, Cindy grabbed the hem and pulled it down before Clara revealed her bra. Clara squashed the blouse into a ball and threw into the trash.

"We can wash the blouse in the ladies' room," Cindy said, taking it from the garbage can. "It'll take only a few minutes to dry under the hand dryer."

"No. It's okay. I have a t-shirt in my locker. Just throw that blouse out. It never looked great on me anyway.

"It's too good to throw out. It's still like new."

"If you like it, keep it."

Cindy unfolded it and held it to her chest. "It's so nice. Are you sure?" She had a wistful look on her face.

"Positive. I really don't want it. It's too blousy and makes me look pregnant."

Cindy stuffed the blouse into her knapsack. "Speaking of pregnant, did you know about your mom and my mom?"

"What about them?"

"Your mom and my mom were friends. They became pregnant at the same time during their last year at high school."

"You mean before they were married?"

"Yes, although my mom didn't marry my dad. Anyway, they thought we might be born on the same day, but I came early. I'm older than you by three weeks. Didn't you know?"

"No way that's true. My mom never mentioned that she knew your mom. Besides, my mother wasn't that kind of girl."

"What kind of girl is that?"

"A slut. My mother isn't like your mother. My mother is a lady."

"If my mother was a slut so was yours. Right, Marty?"

Marty swallowed hard and held up his hands as if to defend himself. "Hey, hey, hey. What do I know?"

"You think you're better than me, but you're not," Cindy said. "Your mother was a slut just like mine. Ask her. It's the truth. I'm surprised she didn't tell you."

"She wasn't, and I'll not have you talk about her like that. You just want to bring everyone down to your level to make yourself feel better."

"My level. And how low is that? We're both mistakes, and no one can change that."

"Shut up," Clara snapped.

"Whoa," Marty said.

"I knew you were lying." Cindy wiped tears from her eyes. "I knew you would never be a true friend. You're just like all the other girls. Just wait until they find out you're trash like me."

"You might be trash, but I'm not," Clara said.

"Hey, let's not do this." Marty tried to place himself between the girls, but Cindy pushed by him and fled the cafeteria.

Marty slung his knapsack over his left shoulder. "Cindy didn't mean to say that. You know she didn't."

"Yeah, I know you're right. God, my birthday is turning out to be a day from hell."

"Oh yeah, I forgot. Sorry. Happy birthday," Marty said.

"No big deal. What's a birthday anyway but a date on the calendar?"

"I like birthdays. Cake and ice cream and everyone treating you as if you're special for one day." Marty scrunched his lunch bag and threw it in the garbage can before leaving through the side door.

They walked across the schoolyard to the racetrack and fell into step in the slow lane. After a quarter turn around the track, Clara broke the awkward silence.

"If my mother was pregnant before I was born, it means my mom and dad...you know." She kicked at the rubberized turf.

Marty shrugged. "So?"

"Cindy was right. I was a mistake. Why didn't they tell me?"

"Hell, I don't know. Your parents love you, don't they?"

"Yeah."

"What's the big deal?" Marty held back a smile. "No family is perfect, Clara. You know all my family secrets. At least your dad married your mom. He did the right thing and has stayed faithful all these years. Look at Cindy. Raised by a single mom. She doesn't know who her dad is, and she's looking to make a connection with you. She needs a friend."

"It's hard because I used to belong to the popular crowd, and now because of her, I'm tagged as—I don't know how to say it."

"Geek, outcast, low class. I've been all those things all my life, and you hang out with me."

"That's different. You have the status of being super smart even if you are a geek."

"Thanks. That makes me feel so much better."

"I know Cindy needs a friend, but the truth is I do feel as if I am better than her. I hate to admit it, but I'm embarrassed to be seen with her. Ever since I promised to help her with her homework and walk her home from school, she's attached herself to me. Like we're best friends or something, but we're not. At least, in my eyes, we're not. Now, because of Cindy, I don't have any friends."

"You stopped being friends with those girls long ago, ever since Peter and you started dating. I don't think it's all Cindy's fault. I think Isabel is your biggest problem. She says nasty things behind your back. She's on a mission to break you and Peter up."

"Is he cheating on me?"

"Hell no." Marty dug the toe of his sneaker into the dirt.

"But something is bothering him. Peter has a secret. Do you know what it is?"

"Peter won't talk to me about it, but I can tell you what I think happened. Do you remember the party at Isabel's house? It was a school night, and her mom was away on a business trip."

"What about it? Peter didn't go, did he?"

"Well, I convinced him to go with me. Ashley was going to be at the party, and—"

"Yeah, I know, you've still got a thing for her."

"When she asked me to come to the party, it felt like—almost a date. I had to go. We're working on a project together, and I thought she was starting to like me for myself, not my brains. Anyway, Isabel was drinking, and she started flirting with Peter big time. Around eleven or so, Peter left the party with her. She said they were going to the corner store to pick up a few more snacks. They took her mom's car. Peter went with her because he was worried that she had too much to drink."

"Was Peter drinking?"

"Not a drop."

"Was he kissing her?"

"Isabel was kissing him a lot. Anyway, about an hour later, everyone had left. No booze, no food, no party. I waited around for a while because I didn't know if I should leave and lock up the place. I didn't know if she had a key to get back in, so I stayed and tried to clean up the mess. It was way after midnight when they returned on foot, without the car. I watched them through the living room window. Peter walked Isabel to the door, but he didn't come in. She had sobered up a bit, but her eyes were red, and her make-up smeared. I wondered if they had fought. When I asked her what happened, she said they had gone for a walk by the river. When they returned to the car, it was gone. I told her to call the police, and she said she had already talked to them." Marty thrust his hands into his jean pockets.

"They went for a walk by the river?" Clara grabbed his arm and whirled him around to face her. "The river?" She said again.

"That's our special place. That's where Peter and I go, and—"

"Make out?"

Clara's face turned the color of Hubba Bubba bubble gum.

Marty took his glasses off and cleaned them on his shirt. "I'm sure it's not what you're thinking."

"C'mon, Marty. I've had a few walks by the river with Peter."

"Well, anyway, the next day, there was something in the news about a hit and run. Later I heard that the person who stole Isabel's parent's car hit a homeless guy. He's in critical condition but expected to make it. But the strange thing is that the story changed. Isabel told the police that someone stole the car while they were at the party."

"If what you're saying is true, Peter and Isabel could be in big trouble," Clara said.

"But he's not talking about it."

"Isabel isn't old enough to drive. She doesn't have a license. She won't turn sixteen until July."

"Yeah, but she takes the car out at night all the time when her mom is sleeping. She's been doing that all year."

"So, who was driving? Peter?"

"I don't know. I didn't see who got behind the wheel. The only good thing is that no one died."

"Still, this is serious."

The warning bell rang for the next block. Marty looked at his watch: 12:20 pm. "You didn't hear this from me. Okay?" He half-walked and half-ran across the schoolyard toward the door.

After kicking a palm-sized rock out of the ground, Clara picked it up and threw it. It landed a few paces from her with a plop.

Anger was the worm gnawing at Clara's gut. I could only guess what she must be feeling. Peter was slipping away from her, and there was nothing she could do to stop it. If she confronted him, she risked making matters worse. All she could do was wait until later, after her audition, when he promised to explain what was going on between him and Isabel. If he didn't come clean, Clara would probably never trust him again. I also knew the longer she had to mull over what Marty said, the worse it became in her mind and the crazier it would make her feel. She would wonder what Peter and Isabel had done on that walk by the river? Did they kiss, and if so, did Peter kiss Isabel the same way he kissed Clara?

Chapter Fifteen

I think Peter's kiss with Isabel was still on Clara's mind when she walked into the girl's washroom because she kept mumbling, "What a bitch," over and over again. She leaned over the sink and splashed water on her face.

"Who's a bitch?" A voice asked from behind one of the bathroom stalls and on the heels of a flush. Clara spun around as Isabel stepped from the stall. She straightened her butt-length denim skirt, walked over to the sink, turned on the faucet, and washed her hands. "Talking to yourself again?"

"No, to you." Clara took a paper towel and dried her face and hands.

"Me? You're calling me a bitch after the stunt you pulled in the cafeteria?" Isabel looked Clara up and down.

"And a slut." Clara threw her wad of paper towels at the garbage can and missed.

Isabel choked back a laugh. "Look who's talking. I heard your mom was knocked up before she got married. Word gets around, you know." Isabel rummaged through her purse and found her lipstick.

"Where did you hear that? Cindy?"

"No, Lana, my dad's ugly girlfriend, Cindy's mom."

"Why would she tell you that?"

"Because it's true, and she knows I can't stand you. Giving me the dirt on your mom was her way of trying to make me like her. That will never happen. I'll never like her or you." Isabel said as she leaned toward the mirror and began to apply her lipstick. To my surprise, Clara smacked the lipsitick out of Isabel's hand. A maroon streak spread from Isabel's lips to the middle of her cheek.

As fast as I'd seen any scrapper in a bar, Isabel spun, and shoulder-checked Clara against the wall, and delivered a sucker punch that knocked the air out of her lungs. "That's for the mealworms," she said.

Clara doubled over, gasping for breath.

I was getting ready to spring into action. If Isabel hit Clara again, I would find a way to kick her ass to kingdom come. It didn't come to that because Clara straightened and slammed the heel of her palm against Isabel's forehead. It snapped back with a crack. Isabel would feel like she had whiplash tomorrow.

"That's for spreading lies about me," Clara hissed.

With the same precision as Isabel would shoot a basket, she scored a hit to Clara's nose. Blood squirted down the front of Clara's tank top. She wiped her nose with the back of her hand and smeared blood from her nose to her ear.

I broke my oath of no interference. I flushed the toilets and turned the automatic hand dryers on all at once, hoping to break up the fight. The distraction worked.

Isabel spun around to see why the toilets and hand dryers had gone crazy. "What the hell?"

Ashley burst into the washroom. "Hey, what's going on in here?"

I stopped the toilets flushing and the hand dryers blowing.

Ashley tiptoed around the blood-spattered bathroom floor. "Have you guys been fighting?"

"Get out," Isabel snapped. "This is between Clara and me."

"Okay, whatever. Mind if I use the loo first?" Ashley pushed open a stall door.

"Flush that piece of shit down the toilet when you're finished." Isabel stormed from the washroom.

With the water on full, Clara leaned over the sink and soaked her nose in her hands.

My brother Jake decked me once. We'd fought over Marie. I remember the awful feeling, the thump, the air sucked out of my lungs, and the taste of blood. My nose didn't break, but it bled like a stuffed pig. It hurt like the dickens too. Oh yeah, and there's nothing like a whack to the nose to give you a shiner.

Ashley flushed and came out of the stall. She stood by the sink and washed her hands. "What was that about?" she asked. "The mealworms?"

"Why should you care?"

"I told you she wouldn't let it go." Ashley handed Clara a wad of paper towels. "Your nose is swelling. I think you might get a black eye."

"Great." Clara took the paper towels and covered her nose. "Now, I'm going to look like the bride of Frankenstein for my audition."

"Wrong play," Ashley said with a modicum of empathy. "I wanted to talk to you about that and…and to offer you a birthday present. I didn't forget, you know."

"I don't want your present."

"You'll want this one."

Clara threw the paper towels in the garbage, looked in the mirror, and groaned.

"It doesn't look broken," Ashley said, "But keep it cold, and the swelling should go down before your audition." She took a small cosmetic case from her purse and pulled out a tube of something I didn't recognize. "Here, you can borrow my cover-up stick."

"What do you want, Ashley? You're never nice to me unless you want something."

"Well, that's what I wanted to talk to you about. You see, I have a problem, and you might be the one to help me. In return, I'll forgo the audition, and you'll get the part by default."

"You'd do that?"

"If you help me."

"With what?"

"I got caught shoplifting. Something small and well now my mother won't pay for my dance or music lessons."

"So? What can I do about that?"

"Talk to my mom. Tell her Tina and Isabel made me do it. Tell her it was their idea, and I was the one who got caught and that I didn't want to do it. Tell her I had to do it because they dared me to. You know how it is. You just have to go along with it to stay popular and have the best friends at the school."

"They're not the best friends, Ashley."

"No, but they're the most popular."

"With the boys, not the other girls."

"It's not easy, you know."

"Tell me about it. I've been on the outside all year." Clara dabbed her nose and winced.

"I'm sorry."

"Sorry isn't enough to get me to lie for you."

"I won't go to the audition. Isn't that enough? I didn't want the part in the first place. I only auditioned for the part because you wanted it. Besides, Julian has the part of Rolfe, the boy who falls in love with Liesl, and it would be a bit weird having to pretend I have a crush on my brother."

"Julian? I didn't know he auditioned."

"Yeah, and he found out last night at the men's call-backs that he won the part."

"Great. It will be awkward for me too," Clara said under her breath.

"Why is that?"

"You don't know?"

"We hardly ever talk anymore."

"A year ago, Julian and I dated once, but it didn't work out." Clara didn't mention the awkward kiss.

"Strange, he never told me you dated. But hey, you're both actors, and you're a year older. You never know. You two could still make a great couple."

"Maybe, but only on stage. Besides, I have Peter."

"Well, yeah, so, anyway, the part is yours if you can help me." Ashley wet a corner of a paper towel and wiped the blood from Clara's nose. "There, that's better."

"If I lie for you, are you still going to hang with Isabel and Tina?"

Ashley squished the bloody paper towels and threw them into the trash can. "I don't know. I liked Isabel at first, but lately, she's been out of control. I'm worried she's going to go too far one of these days, and now after that mealworm stunt, she'll want revenge. You do know she has it in for you and Cindy. The whole idea of her father dating Cindy's mother has made her crazy, and losing Peter to you has put her over the edge. She's pissed you stole him from her."

"I didn't steal him."

"That's not how she sees it."

"Why do you hang with her if you're scared? She's going to get you into more trouble. You're a better person than that."

"I'm not. I've never been as good as you. That's why my mom is always saying, why can't you be more like Clara? That's why I know she'll believe you if you talk to her."

"That's terrible. Mom does that to Lucy and me. It's not right to compare us like that. No wonder you stopped being my friend."

"Will you help me?"

"I don't know."

"It's not a lie, exactly. Isabel and Tina did egg me on. Just think about it."

"I will if you think about doing what's right."

"Yeah, I don't know. I'll think about it." Ashley took a purse-sized tissue package from her bag and handed it to Clara. "Here, use these. They're softer than paper towels. And Clara, don't worry about your swollen nose. The part is yours, whatever you decide."

After Ashley left the washroom, Clara examined her nose in the mirror. She tried the cover-up stick to hide the bruise under her eye, but it made it look worse.

She stuffed the cover stick in her bag, left the washroom, and walked down the hallway. When she turned the corner, she saw Cindy sitting on the floor with her back against Clara's locker. She took a deep breath, stopped, and walked in the opposite direction, then changed her mind and went back to get her books for her next class. "Hey, my blouse looks great on you," she said, faking a smile.

Cindy stood and dropped her sketchbook on the floor. "I washed and dried it with the hand dryer in the girl's bathroom. Is it okay? Does it look as good on me as it did on you?"

Clara fumbled with the lock and opened the locker door. "Oh yeah, it looks way better on you than on me."

Cindy smoothed the blouse over her hips. "You think?"

"Definitely."

"Do you want it back?"

"No, keep it." Clara wiped her nose with the back of her hand and groaned when she saw the smear of blood.

"What happened to you? Your nose is bleeding."

"Sometimes I get nose bleeds. That's all." Clara glanced at herself in the mirror hanging inside of her locker door. She rummaged through her purse for the tissues Ashley gave her.

"It looks like someone hit you because you've got a shiner."

"If you have to know the truth, I bumped it." She dabbed her nose with a tissue and winced. "I dropped my lipstick, and when I picked it up, I slammed my nose against the sink's rim. Embarrassing but true."

Not Clara's most creative lie. I'd heard her do better.

Cindy's frown said she didn't believe her either. "If this was because of me—"

"No, it's Isabel and me," Clara said. "The mealworm sandwich didn't help, but she's been looking for a reason to get me ever since Peter dumped her. She decked me in the girls' washroom."

"I'm sorry."

"Stay clear of her. Okay?

Clara picked up Cindy's sketchbook and studied the portrait of me. "Who is this dude, and why do you keep drawing him?"

Cindy took the sketchbook from her. "I told you."

"C'mon, Cindy. Get real."

"You don't see him, do you?"

"Why would I?"

"He hangs with you a lot."

Clara rummaged in the bottom of her locker and found a black t-shirt rolled up in a ball. She shook it out and slipped it over her head. "You think a ghost is following me around? Let me see that picture."

Cindy tore my portrait from her sketchbook and handed it to Clara, who spread it out against her locker. "You know, I have to admit I did see him this morning. He was standing in my bedroom. I thought I was seeing things but—"

"We both can't be nuts, can we?"

Clara bit her lower lip. "How long has this been going on?"

"On and off all week."

Clara's eyes grew wide. "All week. What does he want?"

Cindy surprised me and took two steps toward me. "Do you have a message for us?" she asked.

"Is he here now?"

Cindy pointed a shaky finger at me. "Yes, he's leaning against the wall."

Cindy was psychically sensitive. I'd have to make sure I stayed out of her way so I merged into the wall.

"Why can't I see him?" Clara asked.

"Well, he's disappeared now. But don't worry, I think he's harmless. And If I were going to have a ghost follow me around, I'd want one that looks like him. He's smoking hot. If you want, we could banish him. My grandma taught me how. Garlic, salt, and a little holy water."

Cool. A banishing. Give it a try, girls, but a banishing isn't going to work on me. I love garlic, and I love salt, and a splash of holy water is just icing on the cake.

"No, that won't be necessary. He's gone now. Right?" Clara placed my sketch inside one of her textbooks and closed her locker. She looked at the hall clock. "We'd better hurry. We're late for our next class. I'm sorry I said those things to you, but I know my mom, and she would never have done that. She just wouldn't. She's so proper."

"Okay." Cindy looked at the floor. "I understand if you don't want to believe me. Mistakes happen to the nicest girls sometimes, and I told you about our mothers because I thought if we had something in common, you'd feel better about me. I thought it made us sisters in a strange sort of way."

Clara scowled. "Look, Cindy, we're not sisters, and if you keep spreading rumors like that, we're not even friends."

Cindy blinked away tears and picked up her books. "Ask your mom. Okay?" With her shoulders slumped and her head down, she walked toward her next class.

"I don't need to ask her because it's not true," Clara called after her. She leaned against her locker and slid down the wall, sat on the floor, and opened her textbook to Cindy's sketch of me.

"Who the hell are you?"

Events were moving forward in a different direction than before. From this point on, I had no idea how the next few hours would play out.

Chapter Sixteen

Clara skipped English, her last class, and her final term exam on Shakespeare's "A Midsummer's Night Dream." When she left the school grounds, I followed her down the path toward Mrs. Kelly's house. Clara knocked on the front door, and when there was no answer, she unlatched the backyard gate. After taking a moment to smell the white roses climbing the side of the house, she rounded the corner and found Mrs. Kelly sitting on the garden swing by the fishpond. The breeze carried Mrs. Kelly's voice, soft and surprisingly true to pitch for her age. I recognized the old hymn, "In the Garden," as my grandmother used to sing it when she did her housework. Mrs. Kelly looked like a child with her flannel nightgown fluttering around her legs and her bare feet swinging in time to the hymn. In one hand, she held a clump of Devil's Paint Brush, a pretty orange weed that I rather liked.

"Hey, Mrs. Kelly." Clara plopped down beside her, causing the swing to rock backward and Mrs. Kelly's feet to rise off the ground.

With glazed eyes, she turned and looked at Clara. I can only imagine how Clara felt to see Mrs. Kelly's expression, fearful and vacant.

"Mrs. Kelly, it's me. Clara."

A brilliant orange butterfly koi, flopped on the surface of the water and caught a black fly. It brought Mrs. Kelly back to herself, and she dropped the Devil's Paint Brush at her feet.

"Oh, my, what happened to your face?" She raised a muddy finger to touch Clara on the cheek.

I have to give Clara props as she didn't even flinch when she felt the cold digit brush a line of dirt across her face. She didn't even try to wipe away the smudge until Mrs. Kelly became distracted by a dragonfly hovering over the fishpond. "It's a long story," Clara said.

"I want to hear all about it." Mrs. Kelly stood and padded her way through the grass toward the backdoor. "Come in, and I'll get you some ice while you tell me what happened."

Clara sat at Mrs. Kelly's kitchen table with her hand covering her nose and tears filling her eyes. She looked around the kitchen at the sink full of dishes, a half-eaten piece of toast on the counter, and two knitting needles sticking upright in the peanut butter jar.

Mrs. Kelly washed her hands before she opened the freezer and took out an ice pack. On the upper rack sat a beeping alarm clock.

"Is everything okay with you?" Clara asked as she watched her wrap the ice pack in a tea towel.

"Yes. Why do you ask?"

"There's an alarm clock in the freezer."

"Oh, that. I couldn't get it to stop ringing today. It usually stops after I put it in the freezer for a while." She handed Clara the ice pack. "Now, keep that ice pack on your nose."

Clara winced as she dabbed her nose with the towel-wrapped ice pack. "It's freezing."

While Mrs. Kelly poured hot water into a teapot, Clara went to the refrigerator and removed the alarm clock from the freezer. She tapped the button on top. The alarm stopped. "Next time it happens, just push this button," she said.

"Oh, I didn't know what that button was used for. Thank you. I'll do that next time." Mrs. Kelly placed the teapot on the table. "Keep that ice pack on. It will take the swelling down. So, tell me, who punched you?" She balled up her fist and feigned a boxing punch. "I hope you gave them a bit of their own for doing that, not that I am recommending an eye for an eye or anything. Or turning the other cheek, for that matter. You only have one nose anyway."

Clara laughed. "That's true. It was Isabel who hit me."

"Why would such a nice girl do that to you?"

"She's not a nice girl," Clara said. "She's angry because Peter and I are dating, and she still likes him a lot. She's become a bully too. Clara pulled the ice pack away from her nose. "Does it look bad?"

Mrs. Kelly sat across from Clara and poured two mugs of tea. "Rudolf would be proud to have a nose like yours."

"Oh, damn her. I have an audition tonight. It hurts to breathe. It hurts to smile. It hurts to talk."

Clara set the ice pack down on the table and picked up the mug. "Mrs. Kelly, I was wondering something. You knew my mother when she was my age, didn't you?"

"Very well. Marie lived next door." Mrs. Kelly picked up her cup of tea and took a sip. She sat quietly for a moment before speaking again. "Now, there were two brothers who both liked Marie and used to fight over her. Twins but so different in personality, one quiet and withdrawn, the other loud and rambunctious. Both loved her. It was hard for Marie to choose between them, but in the end, it was Billy who won her heart."

"You mean Uncle Will?"

"Billy. Everyone called him Billy. Sad the day he died. So sad. Marie married your dad about a month after Billy died. You see, Marie and Billy planned to marry straight out of high school."

"Billy and Mom? He didn't mention they were engaged."

"How could he? He died before you were born. You never met him."

Clara held her head in her hands. "I know. I mean… that's right. Oh, I don't know what I mean. Why did I say that? God, I feel dizzy. I guess I meant that Mom never mentioned it." Clara traced the flower pattern on her napkin with her finger before scrunching the napkin into a ball. "It's weird, but I found a pocket watch today in Mom's desk drawer. The watch had an inscription inside, *To Billy, all my love Marie.* That must have been him. I wonder why she didn't tell me."

Mrs. Kelly closed her eyes. Her head dropped to her chest.

"Mrs. Kelly, are you alright?" Clara shook her arm, and Mrs. Kelly jerked awake. Her eyes fluttered open, and for the second time today, she looked at Clara as if she didn't recognize her.

For a moment, Clara panicked. "Mrs. Kelly, are you okay?"

"Yes, why?"

"You were talking about Mom and Billy, and you dropped off to sleep."

"Did I?" Mrs. Kelly ran a shaking hand through her hair, dry strands of silver. "What did I say?"

"Something about my mom and Uncle Will."

"A noisy boy. He played his music too loud and drove a loud motorcycle."

"A biker?"

"I never liked Billy riding his motorbike with nothing between him and the road but a bit of chrome and leather. He'd rev that engine up and down the street, making the worst racket you could ever imagine at all hours of the day and night. The noise would rattle my windows."

Clara took the sketch out of her notebook and spread it on the table in front of Mrs. Kelly. "Is this him?"

"Why yes. That sketch looks a lot like him. Did you draw it?"

"No, Cindy. She's a talented artist," Clara said.

Mrs. Kelly rubbed her stomach. "Oh my, I have a wicked case of indigestion."

"Can I get you something?"

"Just pass me the bottle of antacids. It's over there on the counter."

By the time Clara opened the bottle and took out two tablets, Mrs. Kelly had fallen asleep again with her chin resting on her chest. Clara stood over her for a moment before trying to wake her. "Mrs. Kelly?"

Her eyes flickered open. She raised her head and rubbed her neck. "Don't forget Lucy knows," she said in a sleepy voice.

Clara frowned and placed the tablets into Mrs. Kelly's hand. "Lucy knows what?"

Mrs. Kelly put the tablets in her mouth and rolled them around a few times before crunching on them. Chalk-like powder-coated her lips.

"Twice now, you've told me that Lucy knows something," Clara said.

"Did I? When did I do that?" Mrs. Kelly wiped her mouth with the back of her hand.

"Just now and …and another time. I can't remember. Oh, I know. When we were at the bus stop. Don't you remember?"

"What bus stop? I didn't see you there." With a shaky hand Mrs. Kelly took a sip of tea. "I haven't been out of this house all week."

"I saw you at the bus stop yesterday," Clara said. "Or was it the day before? Never mind, I must be losing track of time."

"Me too," Mrs. Kelly said. "Sometimes, I can't remember what day it is."

Clara looked confused. So was I. She must have had a psychic bleed through from her previous reality. That would explain why Clara remembered what happened at the bus stop. It can sometimes happen when a person experiences another place and time overlapping with their current reality. Most people shrug off such experiences as a dream or forgotten moment.

"I should go, or I'll miss my bus. I have my audition today. Will you be okay?" Clara said.

"Oh yes. Don't worry about me." With a shaky hand, Mrs. Kelly picked up her cup of tea and took another sip. "Off you go. Break a leg, Clara."

"Thanks, but Ashley's not going, so I think I have this one in the bag. That is if they don't disqualify me for…"

Mrs. Kelly's head dropped to her chest.

"Mrs. Kelly?" Clara whispered.

After folding the sketch and packing it into her bag, Clara walked into the living room, found Mrs. Kelly's shawl draped over her favorite rocker. By the time she had made it back to the kitchen, Mrs. Kelly had slumped over the table. "Sweet dreams," she said and placed the shawl over Mrs. Kelly's shoulders before opening the back door and stepping outside.

She walked across the street to the bus stop and sat on the bench. Three times she stood and stepped off the curb to look for the bus. She looked at her watch, checked the time on her cellphone, and paced the length of the sidewalk in front of the bench several times before sitting and rummaging through her bag. She found the kaleidoscope and the book about Einstein, which she placed beside her. After examining the kaleidoscope, fingering the beads and crystals, she lifted it to her eye and pointed it at me. She turned the wheels. The mirrors caught the sunlight, and to my surprise, I reacted to the sun reflecting in my eyes. The urge to become one with the light was powerful, and I found it difficult to maintain my form. There is such joy in merging with light.

"Beautiful," she said before placing the kaleidoscope beside her and picking up her cellphone. I stood behind her and watched her send a text to Peter: *Waiting for you. The bus will be here soon. Love the Kaleidoscope. Love you even more.*

A few moments later, her cellphone chimed, a text from Peter. She opened it, but before she could read it, her cellphone screen went black. "No," she moaned. "Not now. Why didn't I charge the battery before school?" I wanted to help her by giving the cellphone's battery a short burst of energy, but I had interfered enough.

She looked at her watch. It would be 4:30 pm in ten minutes, and if the bus were on time, it would arrive three minutes later.

"C'mon, Peter. Hurry. You're going to make me late." From over the embankment, twigs snapped, and the breeze carried snippets of conversation.

"She's there…"

"Where?"

"Running through the trees."

"C'mon, this way."

"Hey, we need to cut her off."

Clara stood and used her hand to shield her eyes from the afternoon sun and listened. Did she recognize the voices? I hoped so. When she didn't see or hear anything else, she sat and drummed her fingers on her knee. Her anxiety was contagious. Every time she stood, I looked up the street for the bus with her. Every time she checked her watch, I peered over her shoulder.

I wanted to tell her Cindy was in trouble. I wanted to tell her to listen to her gut, but I couldn't interfere with Clara's journey. She needed to live it and make her own choices. Perhaps I could get away with a nudge here and there, but that was all I dared do. I sat beside her and waited, feeling the tension mounting, knowing that something terrible was happening to Cindy down by the river. For an instant, I cursed the helplessness of being a nonphysical being. I was her watcher and Light-Keeper. I would be with her to the end, but I wanted this day to be over as much as she wanted the bus to come.

A scream rang through the ravine. Clara jumped up, grabbed her knapsack off the bench, and flung it over her shoulder. I watched the kaleidoscope roll to the edge of the bench and stop for half a second before falling on the pavement. I heard the tinkle of shattered lenses as the kaleidoscope rolled back and forth before resting against the bus stop.

Clara half-walked and half-slid down the embankment. A root protruding from the ground tripped her. I caught her, but she slipped through my arms and fell on her hands and knees with a groan. Her watch flew from her wrist and landed under a tussock of Jack Pine rushes where it bounced off a rock. I heard the watch face crack. Lucky for Clara, the crystal sparkled and caught her eye. She crawled under the bush, snatched her watch, and shoved it into her pants pocket.

The sound of voices drifted toward her. She crouched behind a balsam fir covered in sap blisters. Tina and Ashley were at the water's edge near the willow where Peter had carved their names.

"She's here somewhere, hiding in the bushes. If she comes out, we'll see her." Tina squatted and looked under the low-lying branches.

Ashley pulled the upper branches aside. "What are we going to do when we catch her?"

"Beat the shit out of her. What else?" Isabel snatched a willow branch off the ground and whipped it against the tree trunk. She handed the branch to Ashley.

"C'mon, guys, I don't think this is a good idea." Ashley snapped the branch in two.

"What? How can you say that?" Tina tore another switch from the willow. "She deserves it for what she did to me. I can still taste those mealworms."

"And that little tramp's mom stole my dad," Isabel said. "I hate her."

"That's not her fault," Ashley argued.

"Are you with us or not? "Isabel's switch whistled through the air a hair's width from Ashley's face.

She backed up. "I guess, but—"

"You'd better be." Isabel poked her stick into the brushwood. "Show yourself, coward. I know you're hiding in there somewhere."

Clara inched closer, being careful to stay hidden behind the bushes.

Further down the river, Cindy emerged from beneath a clump of elderberry.

"Run," I yelled. I couldn't help myself. It slipped out of me.

She ran toward the log, the makeshift bridge they all used to cross the river.

"I see her. Get her." Isabel caught Cindy's arm and spun her around. Cindy spit in Isabel's face and pushed her away. Isabel cursed while Tina and Ashley took their positions on Isabel's right and left.

Cindy glanced at the log. She was only a few steps away. Could she make it? Would they chase her and push her off the log into the rapids? The current was strong, and if she fell, she would be swept away and thrown against the rocks.

Cindy looked in my direction where I stood on a large flat boulder. Her eyes pleaded with me to help her. I'd done enough, and it wasn't my place to interfere, yet it was painful to watch and heartbreaking to stay silent. "Don't do it," I said.

Isabel thrashed Cindy's legs with the willow branch. Cindy stepped back into ankle-deep water between spikes of rushes and cattails. She clenched her fists, mustering the courage to fight with one of the strongest athletes in the school. With the willow switch, Isabel lashed Cindy again, this time across the face. An ugly welt appeared on Cindy's cheek. She covered the wound with her hand.

"What do you want?" Cindy cried.

"I want you to tell your mother to leave my father alone." Isabel snapped the switch against the rushes narrowly missing Cindy's knees.

Cindy stumbled backwards and grabbed a cattail to keep from plunging into the water. "Why don't you tell your father to leave my mother alone?"

"She's a whore," Isabel growled.

"Takes one to know one," Cindy hissed back.

Isabel waded into the water and grabbed Cindy by the front of her blouse.

Clara ran out from behind the fir trees and screamed, "Get your hands off her." She pounced on Isabel, grabbed her ponytail, and yanked her head back. "You bitch," she said at the same time Cindy uttered the same curse and dug her nails into Isabel's arm.

Isabel gritted her teeth beneath a string of curses that could rival any biker I had ever met. She pushed Clara, who fell backward into the water, and she tore Cindy's blouse as she pulled away from her. Beads of blood dotted Isabel's arm, leaving a bloodied tattoo. Her eyes, glistening with hatred, turned on Clara, who scrambled to her feet.

"Watch out," I yelled. Too late. Isabel punched Clara in the face, cracking her nose. My hand rose in sympathy to my own nose. Clara's poor nose had taken a beating today. Her face wrinkled in pain. I imagined her pain shooting through her jaw, her teeth, and into her head. This fight was turning out to be more vicious than the first. I wanted it to end. I didn't want to see it unfold a second time, but I had no choice but to watch and wait.

Clara cried out and bent over to catch the burst of blood.

But only for a second. She stood, roared, and with a right hook to Isabel's jaw, knocked her backward onto the shore.

I was cheering, "That a girl."

Cindy stepped from the water sobbing and trying to cover her bra with the remains of her blouse, but Tina pushed Cindy backward. She grazed her shoulder on a boulder and grimaced in pain as she rolled to her knees.

"That's enough," Ashley stepped in front of Tina. "Run. Clara, get Cindy out of here."

Clara pulled Cindy to her feet. She stood half-bent over, dazed and gasping for air, with tears running down her cheeks.

"Hurry. Let's go." Clara put a bloodied hand on Cindy's back and steered her up the incline. She grasped saplings to pull herself along, groaning with each slow and painful step. "Faster. Faster." Clara looked over her shoulder. "They're gaining on us."

"C'mon," Isabel said. "They're getting away. We'll be in big trouble if they talk."

"Traitor," Tina screamed and shoved Ashley. Ashley pushed back harder. Tina sprung at Ashley and grabbed a handful of hair while Ashley hooked Tina's leg with her foot and tripped her. Tina fell back and landed butt first in a wasp's nest. A swarm of wasps rose from the blackberry bush and spread out to attack the girls' faces, arms, and legs. Tina's flailing only made the wasps angrier. Screams filled the ravine as the girls scurried up the embankment toward the street. Some wasps made their way toward Clara and Cindy, who were almost halfway up the gully.

Cindy shrieked, "Get them off. Get them away. Get them off me." Frantic, she turned in circles to avoid the wasps from landing on her. "I'm allergic. I'll die if they sting me."

Clara ignored the wasps on her own legs and arms and brushed the wasps from Cindy's back. "Keep moving. Hurry." She pushed her ahead. "I'll make sure they don't land on you."

When they reached the top of the incline, I saw Lucy and Marty running toward them, down the pathway by Mrs. Kelly's house. Marty waved and shouted, "Peter's in trouble."

Clara didn't hear him or the bus which was almost upon them. Cindy ran into the street with Clara following behind her.

"Watch out," I yelled.

The bus driver laid on his horn. The brakes squealed, and an earsplitting scream followed a dreadful thud.

I closed my eyes for half a second and opened them. Shocked faces. Blood. Silence as deep as the void. A trio of screams: Lucy's, Marty's, and a siren. A police cruiser stopped in front of Mrs. Kelly's house. Peter sat in the backseat with his face pressed against the windowpane.

Part Three
Clara

Chapter Seventeen

When I was eleven, my appendix burst, and I almost died. One moment I remember talking to the anesthesiologist about my favorite TV show, and the next, I woke in the recovery room. The time in between was a dreamless black void of nonexistence. Waking on the bench by the bus stop felt like that, like coming to, after an operation. I sensed Billy sitting beside me before I opened my eyes. I don't know why, but every ghostly bone in my body hurt. Was it because I remembered the bus's impact this time? Gradually, Billy's face came into focus.

"It played out the same, didn't it?" I choked back my disappointment.

"Did it?" Billy folded the newspaper and placed it beside us.

"I can't remember if I made a different choice or not."

"Think about it for a minute. Take your time."

"Time? I wonder. Am I out of time, or do I have all the time in the world? Or, as Einstein says, is my perception of time an illusion."

"It's relative, isn't it? To use an old phrase, time is in the eye of the beholder."

Okay, so I searched through all the things in my mind I knew for sure. I must still be dead because here I was sitting on the bench by the bus stop with Billy. I could remember many things, like my arguments with Mom, Lucy, Peter, and Cindy. It surprised me to learn how much I had fought with people during my last day. Oh yeah, and I had a vicious fight with Isabel. I touched my nose. "Does it look broken?"

Billy smiled and touched the tip. "Good as new."

I could remember many things, but I couldn't sort out what happened the first time and what happened the second time. If I could see everything organized side by side, I would be able to sort it out. Right now, everything was a washing machine muddle. But there was one thing I had to know. "Is Cindy okay?" I held my breath and waited for the answer.

"Yes, you saved her."

A terrible weight lifted from my heart. Somehow, I'd made a different decision, the right one. "What did I do? What made the difference for her?"

"Many things, and we all had a hand in changing the course of events."

"You too?"

"Me too. I sat with Cindy in band class, and because she is psychically sensitive, she saw me and drew my portrait. You recognized the sketch because you'd seen me that morning waiting for you in your bedroom."

"That didn't happen before?"

"I was waiting for you, but you didn't see me the first time."

"I didn't go back the same person, did I?"

"No, you didn't. Nothing happens the same way twice. Do you remember what you did the first time?"

I did and the shame burned through me. "I stayed at the bus stop when I knew Cindy was in trouble. Nothing was going to keep me from my audition, not Cindy and not Peter being late. After being stung by the wasps, Cindy climbed up the embankment. She was hysterical, and she ran into the street in front of the bus. I ran after her and pushed her out of the way, but the bus hit me instead. In that reality, I saved her from getting hit by the bus but not from the bullying. Even worse, I didn't save her from the wasp stings which would eventually kill her."

"An unfortunate tragedy that made you feel your death was meaningless. That is why you wouldn't cross. You knew that you had made poor choices. Funny, the drive to succeed is applauded until the drive overshadows the wellbeing of those around us."

"I see that now, but I still don't understand why I made a different choice."

"Seeing me and sharing that experience with Cindy made you kindred souls in a way. You discovered how much you two had in common. The second time around, you had more empathy for her. You came to her rescue and caught her before she stepped into the wasps' nest. Now she will be able to complete something she was destined to do."

That surprised me. I'd never thought Cindy would do anything with her life. I felt a little jealous like maybe she was a better person than me. "What was she going to do? Be a famous artist?"

"Yes, but more importantly, she will paint endangered species of birds and, in doing so, bring awareness to their plight.

A foundation and bird sanctuary will be established in Cindy's name. The interesting thing is that through her work, an almost extinct plant, an endangered bird depends on for survival, will be discovered and found to be important in the development of life-saving medicines."

I wiped the tears from my eyes. "That's pretty cool."

"It is, isn't it? And because of you, she will find success and happiness. She'll marry Marty."

I smiled. I'd always known Marty and Cindy were perfect for each other. "Why didn't Marty wait for Cindy and walk her home?"

"The police delayed him."

"But in the first reality, Marty didn't wait for Cindy either. Right?"

"No, she didn't wait for him because the girls ambushed her. They chased her before Marty arrived at the west exit where they planned to meet."

"Oh, I didn't know that."

"There was no way you could have known."

"And Ashley? Why did she have a change of heart?"

"Remember the ripple effect of one small pebble?"

"Yes, I was mad at you for saying that."

"You are that pebble."

"I don't understand."

"You told her she was a better person, and that caused her to think about her choices and their effect on other people."

Cool. I might have been a small pebble, but I had initiated a big change. I liked that feeling. "And Peter. He didn't come to meet me because the police caught up with him at school. It all makes sense now. Which probable reality will live on? The first or the second?"

"Both. It's about perspective. In one reality, you watched the events unfold for Cindy until the last minute when you jumped in and tried to save her. In the second reality, you became a participant earlier on and changed the timing of events. So, you experienced both realities from two different points in time. Together they exist in the past."

I swallowed the lump at the back of my throat, but it wouldn't go down. It kept creeping up and up. I pleaded with myself to hold it together, but I fell apart when Billy rested his arm around my shoulder. "Why did I have to die, and Cindy live?" I felt ashamed to ask, but I wanted to live and pursue my dream to be an actress. I'd hoped to marry Peter and have children. Why was my life cut short before it had barely started? "Can I go back and try again and create a third probable reality?"

"I loved your mother so much I would have tried and tried to get myself back into her life, but sometimes it's just not meant to be." Billy sighed and took out his pocket watch. He flipped it open so that I could see the engraving. *To Billy. All my love, Marie.*

"You're that Billy?"

He nodded and cleared his throat, visibly moved by his memories of Mom. "Seeing me in your bedroom was the first trigger that sent events on a different path. The pocket watch was the second trigger."

"Mom kept that watch locked in her special keepsake box. I'd only seen it once, a long time ago, when I was sick and stayed home from school. How did it get into her desk?"

"Marie put it there the night she waited for you to come home. She had carried it around with her all day. She planned to tell you when you turned sixteen. When she thought you were old enough to understand."

"Mom gave the watch to you, didn't she?"

"Yes, the night it happened."

"When you died?"

"Yes. It was my fault. I did a stupid thing. We'd gone on a date, and I was driving Marie home. I was impatient with the car in front of us, an elderly couple, out for a Sunday drive on a Saturday night in their maroon Ford Fairlane. Beautiful car. The road was narrow, winding, and lined with pines. I'd seen the sign warning about the sharp curve ahead but ignored it and decided to pass. I had just bought a new hog. It had a lot of guts, and I was itching to see how fast it could go. I floored it. When I saw the station wagon coming over the hill and heading straight for us, I swerved off the road and hit a tree. I died instantly, but it was harder for your mother."

My mother never talked about the lumpy scar that ran up the side of her leg and the one hidden by her bangs. "An accident," she said when I asked her about it.

"My dad's brother's name was William. You're my uncle, aren't you?"

"No, I'm not your uncle, but—"

"You're my father?"

Billy closed the pocket watch and slipped it into his pocket. "You figured it out."

"Why didn't you tell me?"

"What would you have said if I had introduced myself? Nice to meet you, Clara. My name is William Monroe, and I'm your father."

"I see what you mean." Strange how different Billy looked now. The biker dude had become my father. "Why didn't my parents tell me?"

"Your dad asked your mother before they were married to keep it a secret. He wanted you to grow up thinking he was your father, and he was, in every way, a father should be. I'm thankful he raised you as his own with all the love I would have given you.

I'm sad I won't be around for all the important events in your life, to hold you when you're sad or guide you when you need advice. Now, all I can do is be your Light-Keeper and whisper in your ear when you are going the wrong way, cheer when I am proud of you, and hope you can hear me sometimes."

At first, death made me feel like an orphan. Now, I had two fathers, one earthly and one ghostly. I couldn't call Billy angelic because, let's face it, he was a biker through and through.

"What would my life have been like if you had lived to be my father?"

"The same in some ways and different in others."

"How different?"

"Well, we could explore that probability if you decide to."

I thought about that for a minute. "I'd like to do that. Still, I wish my parents were confident enough in my love for them to tell me about you when I was younger." I couldn't hide the disappointment in my voice. "They lied to me all my life, and no amount of love can make up for that."

"Don't be so hard on them. Parents aren't perfect. They all make mistakes."

"Did Lucy know?"

"Yes, Lucy found out that day she caught Isabel kissing Peter. It turns out that Isabel overheard Lana telling Isabel's father and she wanted to know if it was true."

"Isabel was looking for dirt on me."

"Yes, but Lucy wasn't sure if it was true or not. She told Mrs. Kelly because she didn't know if she should ask her mom about it. Mrs. Kelly told her to talk to you first, and together you could talk to your parents."

"Oh…Lucy knows. That's what Mrs. Kelly kept saying."

"It was an odd bleed-through from the first reality, and I have to say I was impressed you remembered."

"Poor Lucy. So that's what she wanted to tell me." I buried my head in my hands. I couldn't bear to think about her. More than anything, I wanted to see her again. I looked around and found the kaleidoscope under the bench. I heard the rattle of glass pieces. "It's broken."

"This is a different reality, Clara."

I walked over to the lamppost, but there was no shrine in memory of me. No flowers or candles or pictures. Freddy wasn't there. It was as if I'd never died. "What will happen to Peter? Will he go to jail?"

"You'll have to ask him."

"When?"

"When you wake up."

"I am awake. Dead awake."

He smiled, picked up the kaleidoscope, and handed it to me. "Look through it."

I looked through the kaleidoscope and saw a mound of glass fragments at the bottom of the hollow cylinder. "There's nothing much to see through a broken kaleidoscope."

"Turn the wheels," Billy said.

When I turned the wheels, two intersecting kaleidoscopic streams of light appeared. Not believing my eyes, I pulled the kaleidoscope away and saw under the streetlamp two roads shimmering like light streaming through fractured glass.

"You are at a crossroads," Billy said. "You can come with me or stay and live out the rest of your life. If you stay, you'll wake up in the hospital."

"You mean I, did it? I'm alive?" I squealed with excitement.

"Your injuries are critical. You're in an induced coma. If you choose to stay, you'll have a long road to recovery. You'll not be able to dance, but you might be able to walk."

"If I can't dance, there's no point in living." I immediately regretted my anger. Of course, life was about more than dancing.

"The road to recovery will be painful and frustrating. When you feel it's too hard, look through the kaleidoscope and change your perspective."

"But the kaleidoscope is broken."

"As you heal, the glass will find new patterns, and the light will always shine through."

I turned toward the lighted paths when I heard the bus come around the corner and stop at the bus stop.

The doors swished open, and Mrs. Kelly stepped out the back door. She walked toward the light streaming under the streetlight. "Don't worry, honey," she said. "When we get home, I'll put the kettle on for tea."

I watched her disappear into the light. "Mrs. Kelly died that afternoon when she fell asleep in her chair, didn't she?"

"Yes."

"I should have stayed with her."

"There was nothing you could do. Mrs. Kelly slipped away gently without pain."

Billy put his helmet on and lifted his leg over the seat of his Harley. "Will you come with me?"

I looked at Billy, the biker, with different eyes now, daughter's eyes. A part of me longed to go with him, but the pull to return to my family and friends was strong. My heart broke, but I shook my head no. "Will I remember you?" Tears pooled in my eyes.

"Maybe, but the memory will be like a dream you can't quite remember. Like sand running through your fingers. Sometimes, when you're quiet, you may recall some of what has happened."

"Will I ever see you again?"

He smiled and kick-started the hog and revved the engine. "You can bet your life on that."

"How will I get home?"

"I'll take you."

"On your Harley?"

He handed me a helmet. "Trust me. There's no better way to travel."

I put the helmet on and sat behind him. My heart raced.

"Keep your feet up. Place them on the pegs."

I found the pegs for my feet and looked around for something to grab. I held my hands in the air. "Where do I…?"

"Hold on wherever you want, the rail, the grab bars, or me."

I didn't feel safe holding the grab bar, so I hugged Billy around the waist. I didn't see him smile. I felt it. "Which way are we going?"

"Let's head out of town. There's an old logging road that follows the river. It's a bumpy ride but nothing my hog can't handle. Are you ready for the ride of your life?"

"More than ready."

With each rev, I squeezed Billy tighter. Mrs. Kelly was right. Billy liked to drive fast, so fast that everything began to blur together.

We roared by Al's Grocery, my school, and the sports arena, and before I knew it, we were on the logging road, by the river. Billy could have driven around the potholes, but he hit them straight on. The largest ones propelled us into the air. Every time we took a sharp curve, I followed Billy's lead, leaned with him, and hoped I wouldn't knock him off balance. I looked at the rapids running dangerously close to the roadside.

He slowed down and stopped at the end of the road.

"A dead end," I said.

"Not quite." Billy pointed at an old wooden bridge.

The bridge didn't look safe to cross. The wood was rotten in places. "Those planks look rickety. There's no way this bridge will hold our weight. Let's go back."

"We can't. We need to cross the river."

Billy drove us back down the road, did a U-turn, and stopped. "Hang on, babe, you're going home." He floored it.

Three-quarters of the way across the bridge, I heard the planks give way and fall into the water. "Billy, no," I screamed as we flew off the bridge and skimmed over the rapids. We landed with a bounce on the opposite shore, our back tire first. I was laughing and crying as he circled the street a few times before continuing down the road. He drove easy now. The breeze rustling by me, the engine humming beneath us, and the warmth of laying my head on Billy's back lulled me to a quiet place. I felt at peace and happy, and I didn't care if I ever got off Billy's Harley. I could ride with him forever.

I fell asleep for a while. I don't know how long because my watch had died, and time had no meaning to me anymore. When I no longer heard the Harley or felt the vibration running through me, I opened my eyes. Everything looked blurry. I reached up to take off the helmet and felt a thick bandage around my head. Someone squeezed my hand. Billy. No, my father. He brushed a tear from my cheek. His tear.

Where was I? I couldn't breathe, and I hurt like I had never hurt before. I wanted to cry out, but something was caught in my throat, a respirator tube.

A Harley idled outside the hospital window. Inside myself, I screamed. I wanted to jump out of bed and run to the window to see Billy one last time, but I was stuck to the respirator, and I had casts on both legs. I put my hand on the respirator tube to pull it free, but my dad stopped me. Tears streamed down my cheeks. I was helpless to do anything but listen to Billy's Harley idling. He revved the engine one last time, his goodbye. I listened to the sound until it disappeared. It's hard to sob when you have something shoved down your throat. My dad tried to calm me. He called for the nurse.

I closed my eyes and saw Billy sitting on his Harley, riding beside the river. He would wait for me at the place where dreams intersect. A blink in time for Billy, a whole life for me.

"You're wrong, Billy," I said silently. "I remember everything."

In my mind, I heard him answer, *Ride-on babe . . .*

Acknowledgements

"Death's Ferryman Ride's a Harley" was inspired by my young adult stageplay, "Kaleidoscope." While the novel has changed significantly from the original play, most of the main characters have remained the same. I would like to thank my drama students Mellissa (Clara), Jarrod (Peter), Zorion (Marty), Breanne (Lucy), Mona Lisa (Isabel), Amanda (Ashley), and Terry (Billy) for bringing my characters to life and giving them a voice that I still hear to this day.

I also would like to acknowledge Ray Hudson, Edna Hudson, Zelda Frost, Kay Johnston and Mary-Lou McCausland for their helpful comments and encouragement.